Our
Eddie

Our Eddie

by

Sulamith Ish-Kishor

PANTHEON BOOKS

The characters in this novel are purely fictional. Any re-
semblance between them and persons living or dead is un-
intentional and coincidental.

The lines quoted on pp. 28, 29 are from *The Fairies*, a
poem by William Allingham. d. 1889).

The lines quoted on p. 95 are from the poem, *Scum of
the Earth*, by Robert Haven Schauffler.

The children of the poor and troubled
rarely do come to full growth; like
forced fruit, they blossom too early and
wither before they ripen.
    Of these,
    For these,
    To these,
    Whatever their age, country, color, or creed,
    This story,
    By one of these.

Sulamith Ish-Kishor

For my sister Penina, with love
and for H. Lee

Our Eddie

I
HAL

ONE

It was strange, the way I first met the Raphel family.

We were living on the same street, but I didn't know it. I was just a kid from the United States, trying out my first cricket bat. I wanted like anything to go out for practice on the Hackney Downs or to Dusty Heap on the River Lea, in northeast London where my Dad and Mom had rented a house. Dad had brought us from the States a few weeks before; his business made him travel a lot, and Mom hadn't wanted to be left home this time.

There was no point in sending me to school. Dad didn't think we'd be staying in London long enough; he had a teacher come to our house every day. So I didn't know any other boys, but there were always some of them playing cricket at Dusty Heap.

Our street was like a lot of other streets in the neighborhood; they were rather new at that time. All the

3

houses were exactly alike—two stories high, little pointed roofs, a basement underneath the house, an ironwork gate in front of the steps, a little garden behind with about enough space for a Wandering-Jew tree in one corner and a small rosebush in the middle.

Summer was beginning. Dad was away.

It was drizzly that day, so I said I'd go to the library on Church Street. Mom said O.K. and told me the muffin-man came around at four o'clock and if I got home by four we'd have toasted muffins and strawberry jelly. They call it jam in London. I loved strawberry jam, so I went early from the library where I used to go and read G. A. Henty's books about boys having adventures in wartime and helping to save the British Empire.

I heard the clock from the Defoe Street church chiming four; (they said Thomas Gray wrote the *Elegy in a Country Churchyard* there; it was the country then) and Daniel Defoe was buried there; he wrote *Robinson Crusoe.* So I was hurrying home, and when I came to Princess May Road I ran, and there was our house, and I ran down the basement entrance and up the little flight of stairs to the kitchen where Mom and the maid Doris would be fixing our tea. Mom liked having English teatime.

But—brother! what was I into!

4

The kitchen was jumping with kids and people!

In the corner was an old black baby carriage with a red-haired baby lying in it and kicking up its bare legs and dragging its fists in and out of its mouth. At the side under the window was a table and there was a kid sitting under it giggling and throwing bits of crust he was chewing all over the floor. There was a big girl with big sparkly light eyes and a red ribbon sticking high up on her hair; she was lifting a kettle off the stove and she frowned at me, wondering who's this? There was a smaller girl with dark, fiery eyes and her hair cut short; she looked sad but she smiled at me. Then there was a lady sitting by the table, cutting a cottage loaf, the round kind with a bun top. The lady was real beautiful, with a lot of wavy, curly black hair all around her head, and large soft brown eyes; her nose was thin and wavy in the middle, and she had rosy cheeks too. You could see she was the mother.

Then a big boy came running downstairs and he came into the kitchen too; he was about a year older than I was,—maybe fourteen even. He looked sun-tanned and breezy, as if he liked outdoor games. He had gray eyes.

"What do *you* want?" he said to me.

"We don't want to buy anything," the big girl with

5

the light eyes said, putting down the kettle on the stove. "You ought to have knocked on the street-door."

"Oh, shut up, Lilie," the boy said.

"Maybe he wants some bread and jam," said the girl with the short dark hair.

"Come here," the mother said, kindly. And she held out to me a thick slice of the crispy side. It was sopping with strawberry jam and butter so that it leaned over in her hand, not all skimpy and polite the way Doris smeared it, so I took it and I had to hold it in both hands and gulp it and it was just the juiciest ever!

"Well, I suppose the poor boy is hungry," said Lilie.

"Children are always hungry," said the mother, and she smiled at me and never told me to watch about dripping it on my clothes, only she took a cloth and wiped off a gob of jam from my shirt. I said, "Thank you, ma'am."

"Oh, Lilie! that boy isn't *begging!*" exclaimed the girl with the short hair. "Look at his nice jacket and britches and shoes!"

"Are you lost?" asked the mother, and she frowned as if she were worried.

"No, ma'am," I said, through the bread and jam.

6

"I guess I walked into the wrong house. I live on this street."

"What number?" asked the big boy.

"Fifty-nine."

"Oh—this is *forty*-nine. The gate's painted green, the same color as yours," he said.

"Olive-green," said Lilie, pouring boiling water from the kettle into some thick white mugs on the table. Then she poured some milk from the pitcher into each cup; the mother and Lilie got real tea from a shiny brown teapot.

"Are you a new boy here?" Eddie asked. He was sitting at the table drinking the hot milk-and-water, with a lump of sugar in it.

"Yes. We just came to London about two months ago."

"You can't play cricket, can you?"

"I've got a cricket bat. You just have to show me."

"Bully! You can join our club. We've got a wicket and stumps. We go over to Dusty Heap every day it doesn't rain after school and in the summer holidays. What's your name? Sit down here." He made room for me at the table, and the dark girl gave me a mug of milk-and-hot-water.

"Hal. Hal Kent. We're from Denver, Colorado . . . What's yours?"

"Eddie Raphel. That's my big sister, Lilie." He nodded his head over toward the older girl. "And that's my younger sister Sybil." This was the dark one. "That's our mother. The baby isn't ours; we're minding it for a neighbor."

Mrs. Raphel smiled again.

"Our father's a teacher," said Sybil. "He's a headmaster. Of the Hebrew school in the East End." She sounded proud of it and not proud of it, at the same time.

"You needn't tell everybody everything the first time you see them," said Lilie.

So I went home and explained to Mom how I'd gone into the wrong house and met another boy. She was kind of angry because I came home late and she didn't know where I was. But she was pleased that I'd met a nice family on the same street.

One thing I liked at the Raphels,—there was always some sort of excitement. And then sometimes, if Mrs. Raphel was feeling cheerful, she would tell stories, about her life in southern Russia, and the great orchards on the big estates, and how enormous the fruit was. Her face would get rosy and young when she talked, her eyes would sparkle and she smiled a lot. She had hardly any foreign accent, and she spoke English fine.

"Cherries," she said, picking up a bowlful that someone had brought in. "These, cherries? They should see *those* cherries! Large as your plums, and rich, juicy!"

"Did they have other fruits there?"

"Apples, pears, plums, melons—what did they not have! Grapes—the world was full of them! And for two kopeks you could go in and eat till you burst! Only you mustn't carry any away. Still, some people hid them in their pockets or under their skirts—well, no one minded that, but they mustn't carry bags. And in spring—Ah! in spring, when all the blossoms were out—cherry blossoms, apple blossoms, plum blossoms, for miles and miles, clouds of blossoms pink and white—and the fragrance—!"

She told us about the parties when she was a girl— the wild dancing of the gypsies and the peasants. Then she would sing songs, all in Russian, songs of heartbreak, and stories in music, like one about Napoleon exiled all alone to the isle of St. Helena, and about a lover who killed himself for a scornful beauty who calmly stepped over his heart, or something like that; she would tell us the story of the song after she sang it. Her voice was low and had a real zing to it, and while she was singing you'd think she really felt that way; sometimes there'd even be tears in her eyes, but afterward she'd laugh. It was fun when she sang.

I went over to the Raphels a lot. I didn't meet Mr. Raphel for a long time; he taught evening school in the East End where the people were quite poor, and he had to be there by three o'clock in the afternoon and he didn't get back till late at night.

I used to come over after school, about teatime. Mrs. Raphel never said I couldn't. She was always home, and she would cut me a real thick slice of bread and butter and really pour the jam on it; sometimes it was black bread and that was twice as good! but that was Mr. Raphel's bread and the kids didn't often get it. At home Doris still cut those slices like paper you could see through. She didn't think a real slice was polite, and even with muffins she would only sort of smear the knife across it with jelly on. I never did like that Doris. And Mrs. Raphel put a spoonful of real tea in my milk-sugar-and-water.

My Dad only came home weekends that summer; he was head of a sales department for American General Foods Canning Company, and he had to open new territory all the time. So he had to travel around a lot. He was smart and he made out fine.

One day I was sitting in our garden, ha ha; it was about as big as your grandmother's handkerchief; it was just before dinner time and I was reading a new Gem Library story about boys in an English public school (that means paying-school in England) and I couldn't figure out their angle, and I heard Mom and

Dad arguing upstairs from the bedroom window. Mom was saying she wanted to go back to the States, and then they were talking about the Raphels.

"Oh," Mom was saying, "I don't agree with you there. I went to see Mrs. Raphel and I never did see such a house. All helter-skelter and hobble-de-hoy! Land o' Goshen! Eleven in the morning and the beds weren't made and the kitchen—just a mess of kids and food. If you want Hal to—"

"I don't want Hal to be a fussbudget like you, and that's the way he's getting here! He's a *boy!*" Dad was tall and big and his voice always sounded important. "This place is a regular doll's house on the side of a wall with that Doris. You don't need everything spick and span every minute—"

"Oh, very well, Mr. Kent!" I knew then that Mom was mad with him. "In the future I'll sit with folded hands and let—"

"Now you're off again. You'll have that boy grow up a sissy. I want him playing outdoors with other boys. We can't put him in school here, he'll only have to be dragged out again in midterm. No brothers or sisters. *He* needs the Raphels. *They* don't need him."

"The way they argue all the time—"

"Let him see how other people live!"

"I don't think the father—"

11

"The father's a teacher, isn't he? Gets his bellyful of kids all day; what do you expect when he gets home?"

Then they shut the window and I couldn't make out the words any more. I figured he meant we'd be going back to the States by Christmas. I never said anything. It wouldn't have made any difference, because that was business.

But I was glad Dad wasn't going to let Mom interfere with my going over to the Raphels while we were here.

TWO

I didn't like all the Raphels the same.

Eddie was my chief friend because he was only a
year older than me, and he was a right guy. He had a
kid brother that was a lot younger, and was he a pest.
His name was Thad, for Thaddeus. He was always tag-
ging after our team when we went to Dusty Heap or
the Downs, and we couldn't slow down to him and he
couldn't keep up to us. I was kind of sorry for him.
One afternoon when we finished playing cricket we
didn't see him around, and when we got home to the
Raphels' house he wasn't there either.

Then Lilie said,

"Where's Thad?"

Eddie was washing up in the bathroom so I said,
"Thad didn't come with us today."

Syb was suddenly there; her eyes got very big and
her mouth opened and she said,

"Oh, Hal—he isn't anywhere here."

Now Eddie came down. "Ma," he called, and he sounded real mad, "you remember that copybook I lost? I just found it—under the *bathtub,* all wet and dirty! I'll have to copy the stuff out all over again! I'll bet it was that Thad! Wait till I get my hands on him!"

"Oh, Eddie," Syb said, "Thad's lost! He went after you to Dusty Heap—I saw him trying to catch up— he was wearing his red woolen tam—"

"Good job if he is," said Eddie, grabbing a piece of buttered bread off the table and beginning to eat it.

Mrs. Raphel was sitting at the kitchen table and she stopped cutting bread. She turned quite pale and still, and her hand with the knife lay on her apron on her knee.

"Lilie," she said, faintly, "run to Papa's school. Tell him to come home. Eddie—go find a policeman."

"Oh, Ma, Thad isn't lost," said Eddie, irritably. "I'm hungry, and so's Hal. Give us our tea. Thad'll be along in a minute. If he went after us, he must have followed us home, too."

"You didn't see him at all, on the Downs?" asked Lilie, frowning.

"We weren't on Hackney Downs, we were at Dusty Heap."

"That's by the River Lea," gasped Syb, frightened.

14

Mrs. Raphel stood up, her face all white. "Oh—my child! my child! He's been drowned!" She began to cry and scream. "Oh—my little boy! Oh! Oh! my boy—"

"I'll go back to Dusty Heap, ma'am," I said. I began to feel it was my fault, too. "I'll find him."

"I'll go and fetch Pa," said Lilie, and ran upstairs. Eddie stopped munching his bread and cheese.

"I don't believe anything happened to that kid," he said, but his voice shook.

Lilie came back in, with her hat and jacket on.

"Hal," she said, "I think *you'd* better go to the school and get our father. I'll go to the police. You know where Shacklewell Lane is?" She fumbled in her purse. "It's the East End—"

"I take the bus on Kingland Road," I said.

"I'll give you back the fare—." Her fingers were shaking too much to get out the pennies.

"That's all right," I told her. "I've got pocket-money."

"Then Eddie will go to—to Dusty Heap. I'm sure—" She didn't finish; everybody was nervous now, and poor Mrs. Raphel, she was trying to keep her mouth still, but it kept trembling and the tears kept jumping from her eyes, and she was frowning, but it wasn't really a frown.

I walked up to the top of the street and came into

Kingsland Road and there was a bus pretty soon, and I got on it and asked the conductor to let me off near Shacklewell Lane. It was one of the new electric buses, without horses, and it was only the second time I had been on one. I asked the conductor a lot of questions about what made it run; he was a nice guy and he answered me. He asked me where I was from and I told him the United States; he grinned and said, "Oh, really? I'd like to go there one of these days, fight some Red Indians!—Here you are, my lad. Shackle-well Lane."

I got off and found the little school, down the street. It was a very crowded and lighted-up sort of neighborhood, though it was still very light, only 6 p.m.

There was a big boy in the entrance; it wasn't really as large as a lobby. He wore a little round cap on the back of his head. He spoke to me in a thin, sing-song voice, and in a language I didn't know. Then he asked me in English.

"What d'you want in here, eh?"

"Mrs. Raphel sent me. Is Mr. Raphel in?"

He looked surprised, went inside. Then he came out.

"Mr. Raphel's teaching a class."

"But his little boy's lost," I explained.

He went in again. This time he took a lot longer. Then he came out.

16

"You gotta wait." He began folding papers and stuffing them inside envelopes on a desk.

There was a clock on the wall and it was half past six when the doors opened again. Some kids came out, and there was a man with them whom I guessed was Mr. Raphel; something about the way he looked like the Raphel family. The kids were smiling the quiet way you smile with teachers if you like them, and one or two of the little girls were catching at his hands and holding them. He seemed quite pleased and kind. He talked to the big boy first and then he said good night to the kids and they went off and waved goodbye to him.

I figured he was a teacher anyway, so I stood up when he came up to me. He frowned.

"What nonsense is this?" he snapped. "Why have you come here?"

"Mrs. Raphel sent me," I kind of stammered. He wasn't a very tall man but rather broad-shouldered and his eyes were looking real angry, clear through me, snapping gray or blue, very deep-set. His hair was black and combed back over a high square forehead, like one of those engravings of dead people who wrote hard books.

"My wife has no right to disturb me when I am in my school!"

17

That made *me* angry, somehow.

"Your child's lost, Mr. Raphel!" I said.

"When I am in school, *these* are my children!—Tell Mrs. Raphel I will be at home in an hour." He was turning to march away, then he suddenly asked, "Which one is it?"

"Thad."

"Oh!" He shrugged his shoulders and turned around. "He is always playing tricks." He went right in at the door and it slammed shut behind him.

I knew Mr. Raphel was a very intelligent man, real brilliant, people said. But I was glad he wasn't *my* father.

I took the bus back to the Raphels'.

I rang the bell and they opened the door. Sybil opened it and she was smiling. She ran ahead of me into the kitchen, and there Thad was, sitting at the table, while Mrs. Raphel stroked his head hard and Lilie fed him small pieces of meatball with a fork.

Thad was grinning all across his round face, a kind of show-off grin, and there was a mischievous, satisfied look in his big black eyes. He was talking. He didn't have his front teeth yet and he couldn't say "s" properly.

"So then the poleethman he athed me, did I get lotht. So then he athed me where wath my cap. So

18

then I told him, I put it in the river. I want a real
cap like Eddie wearth."

Thad suddenly stopped talking, and then we looked
around and saw that Mr. Raphel had quietly come in.
He was standing there, looking at Thad.

"So that's why you threw the red tam in the river.
The police showed it to me when I went to the Station."

Mr. Raphel spoke calmly, but Thad began to twist
the lock of brown hair at the top of his forehead.

"I knew this was one of your tricks. You went there
to throw away the tam. Then you waited till Eddie
went home, and then you tried to follow, and that's
how you got lost." He went up to Thad, grabbed him
by the collar and pulled him off the chair. Thad began
to yell.

"Let the child alone!" Mrs. Raphel exclaimed.

Mr. Raphel pulled the kid away and dragged him
out of the room. "I'll show you how to make a fool
of me!" we heard him saying. Then a door slammed
and Thad began squealing, "But I *wath* lotht, Papa!
I *wath* lotht!"

We could still hear the spanking sounds and Thad
yelling. Then the door opened again and the kid came
out bawling at the top of his voice, his mouth a
square-shaped hole; his face was red as a tomato and

big tears pouring down and he held both his hands over his backside as he ran to his mother. She put out her arms to him but Mr. Raphel, standing there in the doorway looking very stiff and bossy, called out,

"Do not console him! He will play this trick again if he finds that it pays!" Then he said,

"Ed! Come here. It is your turn now."

Eddie turned red with surprise.

"Me? What did I do?"

"I ordered you to come here!" Mr. Raphel had shut his eyes hard and stood, sort of threateningly waiting.

Eddie went slowly up to him. Mr. Raphel grabbed him by the collar and pushed him in front of himself into the other room. We heard sounds like the strokes of a stick. Mrs. Raphel stood up, her eyes full of tears, biting her lips. Lilie whispered,

"I suppose it's because Eddie wasn't watching Thad."

But Syb turned her head away; her eyes were big and angry.

I ran out and went home. Maybe Mr. Raphel was wrong or maybe he was right, the way grown-ups think. I couldn't figure him out, because I remembered how the school kids hugged his hands and looked at him as if he were some kind of hero.

But I felt sure that I would never like Mr. Raphel.

20

THREE

One Sunday morning not long afterward I knocked on the door of 49 Princess May Road. I had on my everyday knickers and a gray Scotch wool sweater instead of my Sunday Norfolk jacket, because it was Eddie's birthday and the Raphels had invited me to go with them on an outing to the country, not far from London,—Chingford Forest I think it was called.

My Mom and Dad wanted to visit some business friends that day, and they were glad I could go and have a holiday with other youngsters. I brought Eddie a G. A. Henty adventure book for his birthday present.

It was still good weather, though a bit crisp, getting on toward autumn. Our maid, Doris, packed lunch for me, Dad handed me my bus and train fare with a bit extra for treats, and I went off.

Syb opened the door; she gave me her quick, dark smile, that always seemed to have something sad behind it. I liked *her* the best. No one was ready, of course; the little kitchen was full of Lilie and Eddie and Thad and Mrs. Raphel and Ada, the woman who sometimes came in to help.

Mr. Raphel was sitting grandly in the comfortable corner seat at the table against the wall, finishing his glass of lemon tea—it was Russian tea and he held the sugar in his mouth and sucked the tea through it, as they used to do in Russia, they told me. Mrs. Raphel was bending down near the open fire of the stove, holding up to the heat a three-pronged twisted wire toaster with a piece of bread speared on the prongs; one of her cheeks had the sort of rough red flush you get from standing near a fire. Mr. Raphel looked up from his folded newspaper and said, "Make it browner." So she held it a bit nearer the fire. Then she pulled it off and tossed it quickly onto Mr. Raphel's plate; then she put butter on it, and he ate it.

Lilie was putting on a straw hat in front of the unframed looking-glass on a shelf. She took it off, put it back another way, then simpered in front of it, giving me side glances, and said, bunching her full lips together as if she were kissing,

"Sybil, is this hat becoming to me?"

"Oh,—you're not going to a party!" Syb sniffed. "It's all right enough. Why do you bunch your mouth like that? It looks silly."

22

Lilie turned red and snatched off the hat.

"Listen how she talks to me! Mama, make Sybil behave to me!"

"Why do you talk to her like that, Sybil?" Mrs. Raphel exclaimed. "Lilie's your big sister!"

"Well, why does she ask me, if she doesn't want me to tell her? She's always posing. Do I have to pretend I like it?"

Lilie began to cry, and ran out of the kitchen, giving me a strong look as if to say, "See what Sybil's really like?" But Sybil never claimed to be anything she wasn't. She always said what she thought. And besides, Lilie *was* always posing. She wasn't bad looking at all; she had big sparkly light eyes that were sometimes real blue, and shiny wavy reddish-brown hair; her mouth was kind of big and toothy but it was all right, and she never put any paint on. But she made the boys sick with all that pretense. Syb wasn't really pretty except when she smiled, but somehow we all liked her. She didn't talk to us boys as if we were some kind of different animal from girls.

Thad was squatting on the floor, holding a shammy rag and shining Mr. Raphel's boots. I knew they weren't Eddie's because Eddie's were worn all down to the iron blakeys.

"Here, Papa!" Thad scrambled up and put the boots between Mr. Raphel's stocking feet. Lilie came back in; she was calm now and carrying Mr. Raphel's jacket. Thad banged his head against the tabletop as he was getting out from under; he opened his mouth to yell, but decided not to.

"Here, Papa, your boot-th. I bruthed them two times. Now will you take me with?"

Mr. Raphel, accepting another piece of toast which Mrs. Raphel had browned and buttered, ate it, and did not move his eyes from his newspaper.

"Papa, papa, now will you take me with?"

Mr. Raphel still paid no attention. Thad, taking silence for consent, ran out of the room and came back with his cap on,—no hated red tam any more, but a boy's cap, new, and of black cloth with a shiny black peak. He wouldn't let them take the price tag off. He moved the cap proudly from one side of his big tousled head to the other, his black eyes gleaming with joy.

Now Mr. Raphel wiped his black walrus moustache and folded his newspaper. He stood up, pushed one foot into his boot, then the other, and stamped down the heels. He accepted the jacket Lilie handed him, and put it on over his waistcoat, then he came out and stood in the middle of the kitchen.

"Come on, Papa," said Lilie, a bit nervously.

Mr. Raphel beamed a smile all around.

"Guess what," he said. "I have had an idea."

"What idea?" Lilie asked.

"A better way to spend Sunday."

"O-oh," groaned Eddie, standing there, bat in hand.

"An excellent place for a picnic. Very near by. There will be no expense for carfare or refreshments."

There was silence. In sheer puzzlement I put in, "Where would that be, Mr. Raphel?"

He was waiting for someone to ask.

"49 Princess May Road. In the garden."

"That's *here!*"

"Mr. Raphel," put in Ada, who came in to help, "there's a fine bit of roast chicken for you in the lunch box."

Everybody was standing as if frozen.

"I was afraid of this," whispered poor Mrs. Raphel.

Mr. Raphel was smiling around at everybody.

"You're joking, Mr. Raphel," I couldn't help saying. I couldn't believe it. But they knew. Thad opened his mouth till it was a large square, and howled.

"Papa! After you promised us!" exclaimed Lilie, tragically. "It's Eddie's *birthday,*—and you wouldn't let me make a birthday party, because we had this instead!"

"Papa, I bruthed your thoes!" wailed Thad.

Mr. Raphel changed his manner. He was all business. He snapped: "I have a meeting today at school. At twelve o'clock."

25

"Why didn't you tell us before?" Eddie growled. "And you were supposed to have a talk with me, about my future."

"Future! You are fourteen today. We have plenty of time to discuss your future!" Mr. Raphel put on his hat. "I am going now to the school. You may do as you like."

"Papa! Give us our carfare, we can go by ourselves." It was Lilie who spoke. Mr. Raphel looked at first as if he were going to refuse, but there was something resolute in Lilie's voice, and Mrs. Raphel was looking at him in a way—half grim, half about to tell him her mind—and after all, I was there, a stranger. He put his hand into his pocket, took out his change purse, and carefully counted into Lilie's palm some pennies and a couple of shillings. He looked at Thad, who was preparing to howl again, then said, "Thad is half-fare," and took back a penny. "Is your friend included?" He never called me by my name.

"Of course!" said Syb hastily.

"I have my own fare, Mr. Raphel."

"No, you shan't—" Syb began.

But Mr. Raphel had put the amount, including only theirs, into Lilie's hand. "It is useless expense," he muttered.

Still, the day didn't go badly. The weather was fine. I for one didn't miss Mr. Raphel, and I don't think anyone else did. Mrs. Raphel was staying home and wouldn't have come, anyway. She never went out, as far as I could see; she said she was always afraid of something happening to the children if she were away.

It was fun, going on that tiny train, and it was a real, forest-like place when we got there, not like our great, huge, "forests primeval" in the United States, of course, but friendly, with groves of broad-branched trees, big, old trees with lots of deep, grassy spaces around, hollow trees where you could climb up and sit, two or three kids at a time, and all kinds of birds were singing.

There was one very large old oak tree, Lilie said it was a thousand years old; it had lots of spreading green branches, and all of us began climbing up into it, and sat there, except Lilie; she sat on a fallen log nearby and spread out her skirts around her. We got down, Eddie and I played catch and practiced cricket with a branch stuck in the ground, and Thad ran after the ball when it went too far.

Syb was sitting on the grass near Lilie and reading bits of poetry to her. I've always liked poetry and I heard some of it when I stood by them resting a while. And I noticed that she read some of it from a paper notebook and I had never heard it before. She began one:

"Above the world, and history, and time,
Upon a final precipice of thought—"

"Say, where is that from?" I called over to her.
Syb shut the notebook hastily.

"Oh, it's something *she* wrote," said Lilie, crossly.

"Let's have lunch," said Sybil. So I saw she didn't want to talk about it.

Syb began opening the lunch basket, but Lilie called out, brightly, "Let's make a fairy ring! Everybody pull up grass and pile it up!" She began to recite while we pulled grass. I forget the exact words but they were something like this:

> Up the airy mountain,
>   Down the mossy glen,
> We daren't go a-hunting
>   For fear of Little Men—

"That's fairies," she explained—

> Wee folk, good folk,
>   Trooping all together,
> Green jacket, red cap,
>   And white owl's feather.

> They stole little Sybil
>   For seven years long—

"I can't remember what comes here—"

They thought that she was fast asleep,
But she was dead of sorrow—

"Little *Bridget!*" exclaimed Sybil, quite annoyed. "The girl they stole was Little *Bridget!* Why do you always say it 'Sybil' when it's Bridget?"

"Oh, all right! Can't I make a mistake without being a criminal?" Lilie retorted. "Here, now—take the grass, spread it all around us. No, Thad, not around each one,—in a big, wide ring around us all, see, so we'll all be sitting inside the fairy ring."

"Kid stuff," Eddie mocked, but we did it that way.

"Now," Lilie explained, "we're protected in case the fairies come. They can't cross into a fairy ring. So don't jump out of it without saying a charm, and you won't break the spell."

"What would happen if we did?" I wanted to know.

"Oh," said Syb, mysteriously, but she smiled, "something bad might happen. One of us might be stolen away!"

"They wouldn't take *me*," said Thad, sturdily, while Lilie distributed the sandwiches. They were good, with lots of chicken-liver-and-hardboiled-egg, or thick cheese, or sliced meat—we had to eat the cheese ones first because cheese is made from milk, and we had to

29

drink our milk first, and after that we had to drink water with the meat. That's the law for kosher.

"If they took *you*, they'd bring you back quicker than a flash," grinned Eddie, eating his meat sandwich.

"Eddie—you can't have cheese now"—Lilie began, but Eddie calmly picked up a cheese sandwich and began to eat it.

"We could get three wishes for taking him back!" teased Syb.

"One wish would be for the fairies to keep him," said Eddie. This got Thad all confused, and he didn't say any more. Then we gave Eddie his presents, and he was very pleased. Lilie had knitted him a gray scarf, Sybil had three white handkerchiefs with E, and Thad promised to shine Eddie's boots every Friday. Lilie sang a lot of jolly folk songs after that, while we cleared up the litter and stuffed it all into the lunch basket to throw away later. They had wanted to give me Mr. Raphel's roast half-chicken but I wasn't so hungry and I made Eddie and Thad take it. Doris had given me some sliced cake to take along but they were such skimpy pieces I wouldn't offer them, and they all crumbled in my pocket. I wonder why Doris was like that. It wasn't *her* food!

Lilie sang "The Raggle-Taggle Gypsies O," and "Dabbling in the Dew," and "Sir, she said," and then some sad, wild ones, like "Across the Sands of Dee," and "All Through the Night." She was real good at it; her voice was all right too, not zingy like Mrs. Raphel's, but nice-sounding, and she kept in tune. Ada had put the lemonade in a bottle with the cap on tight and Eddie had to hack at the lid with the cricket bat, while Thad held a cup underneath it to catch the spill, but of course it spurted all over him. But there was enough left for everybody to have a drink. We had kept it in a tiny stream nearby so it didn't get warm.

It was a good day.

I'll always remember it because it was the last whole day we spent together. The way things turned out, it was my folks who stayed in England and Eddie's family went to the United States!

My Dad was sent off to Glasgow, to start a branch of the firm in Scotland. When I said goodbye to the Raphels, we thought it would only be for a few months, and then I'd be back in London.

But Dad got sort of settled there in Glasgow. So I wrote to Eddie now and then, and he wrote back. Then he wrote me that they were going away, to New York. Then a long time passed, and we got out of the habit of writing. It wasn't the same thing, anyhow, as seeing them. I really missed them. The Scotch kids were all right but I'd gotten used to the Raphels.

About two years later, Dad decided to go back to

the United States for good. I was glad and I wrote to the old address I had for Eddie, on an old postcard I had kept from him, to tell him that finally we were all going to meet again. But nobody answered me.

II
SYBIL

FOUR

I am Sybil.

And I want to tell the rest of it myself, because I don't want to forget how it really happened.

It wasn't Eddie's fault he did the things he did, and maybe it was only important because he must have felt that he did wrong. And yet he felt that it was not wrong, because nobody had done for us what other parents did for their children. And feeling two ways about what you do, or feeling two different ways about the same people, especially your family, makes you very confused and nervous.

Sometimes it doesn't matter how much money comes in to a family week by week, and sometimes it does matter very much. You have to have enough, anyway. But somehow Papa never could earn as much as other people, even though teaching is such special work, and he was really great in his knowledge and in his methods too. It was almost as though he was afraid of having money enough.

I remember that one morning Lilie got me up early—it was a Sunday—and told us we had to tidy up the parlor very quickly.

The parlor was tidy, really; it was on the second floor and it was a large room with folding doors into Papa's and Mama's bedroom. Nobody ever went into the parlor; it had white lace curtains at the windows, and stiff red plush furniture; the best was a beautiful little writing desk with carved legs, a black Morocco leather lid, and inlays of different kinds of fine wood. The father of one of Papa's pupils had given him this desk; they were very rich, and this boy did not want to learn Hebrew, and would never listen to anybody. But Papa had changed all that, and the boy had learned so well that he surprised the whole Jewish community with his understanding and knowledge when he made his Bar Mitzvah in the grand new synagogue of the West End.

So we dusted off the furniture and I shined up the little desk; it was so gratifying to see the splendid curves and lines of the design come up out of the film of light dust, and the colors, golden and cherry-red and black, deepen in the inlays.

Then Papa came out of his bedroom, all dressed up as if for the annual meeting of his Board, but it wasn't that. We were going to have visitors—that is, Papa was.

Mama was all excited, but Papa told her she must not be present, nor must any of the children.

"You could introduce Mama," Lilie said. "I'll make her look very nice."

"No," said Papa. So that ended it.

When the knock on the door came, Eddie went and opened it. There stood two very important bearded gentlemen. They wore dark, plain clothes that somehow looked very costly and fine; they wore those tall, round silk hats, all black (Papa had one, too, for special occasions; it was kept in a round white box, and there was a thick little green velvet pad to brush it smooth). They had heavy gold watch chains across their stomachs, and they had velvety spats on their polished shoes.

Eddie took their gold-headed canes and their fine gloves, and led the visitors up to the parlor. Then he ran back to the kitchen, and we all waited.

In about half-an-hour the gentlemen came down again, followed by Papa; Eddie handed them their canes and their gloves, they spoke politely to him for a minute or two, then they left.

"What happened, Papa? What did they want? What they say?" We all crowded around Papa, for we had a pretty good idea that it had to do with future benefits.

But Papa shook his head angrily, and went upstairs. Mama followed him. When she came down, alone, her face was pale and her eyes looked angry and hopeless.

"What was it, Ma?" exclaimed Lilie, anxiously.

"Total disappointment," said Mama, dramatically.

She explained. The gentlemen were representatives of the richest Jewish community in London. They had come to offer Papa the head mastership of a new institute of Hebrew learning that was about to be opened. The salary they mentioned stunned us even to hear.

And Papa had refused.

"Why? *Why?*" Lilie wailed.

"He told them, 'It is not the children of the rich who need me, but the children of the poor.' "

It sounded so noble, and we wallowed in the wonder of it—being, I think, unable to understand the difference that salary would have made in our lives, for we were not used to money and it did not seem real to us. We exulted in the incredulous astonishment which our father's nobility must have achieved in these smug gentlemen.

But Mama cried all day, and little by little, as we

realized what Papa had done to us, we began to feel
as if we had lifted a golden goblet to our lips and had
drunk a golden foam and nothing more.

Lilie told me later that she had asked him,

"But why did you let them come, if you knew you
would refuse the offer?"

Papa had said, "I had hoped that I might be able
to persuade them to do a more truly useful thing,—a
more sincere and necessary thing,—to make a solid
contribution to educate all these poor Jewish children
of London. I haven't got room for a tenth of them,
and our old building is falling down. What I asked
for wouldn't cost a hundredth part of what their new
school will cost, and it did *not* include any raise of
salary for myself. They wouldn't hear of it."

So we never got any of the things we wanted. I
wanted so badly to have a white dress; even the poor-
est girl in our school had one. And Eddie wanted a
watch. Papa promised him a watch if he won a scholarship to secondary school. He won it, but he never
got a watch. And Papa promised one of his books,
Josephus' *History of the Jews*, to the child who
would read it first. But when he saw I was nearly
halfway through it—I loved it—he took it away and
gave it to Eddie, who didn't want it at all, just because Eddie was a boy!

Hal went away about this time, and I felt it badly. I was more sorry than I had thought I would be when he first told us they might go. They were supposed to go back to the United States, I knew, but that was not to be till Christmas, and in summer that sounded like almost never. Now they were not going such a distance, only to Scotland,—though as far as we were concerned it might have been three thousand miles. And they were going in a few days.

He said goodbye to us all, in his pleasant way, shaking hands with everyone, even with Thad, whose face twisted up as if he were going to cry. Hal was nicer to Thad than we were, but then he didn't have to have him around all day. He used to bring Thad bulls eyes and strings of black licorice, and talk with the kid the same way he talked to us.

It gave me a strange feeling—a kind of squeezed feeling at the pit of my stomach, when he came up to me and smiled, and I knew it was the last time I would see him, perhaps for always. He was a big boy for his age, with blond-brown hair, and large eyes, light blue and always calm. I couldn't recall him getting into a temper over anything. He was rather a quiet boy, but thinking-quiet, or noticing-quiet, not dull quiet. He never talked about what he intended to be when he grew up; he simply said he had not decided. He didn't talk very much at any time, but he was always "with" you. He was really "a bit of blue sky" to us all, something from the world outside our house, and it was bitter and depressing that he was going away. Eddie looked very gloomy about it, even when Hal told him the club could keep the cricket bat.

I was quite surprised when after he had shaken hands with all of us, he came up to me again and gave me a little kiss on the cheek. Then he went out of the door and down the steps. Mama had tears in her eyes.

But I felt warm and quite pleased about the kiss.

As soon as he had gone, Lilie exclaimed, "Well! If he'd done that to me, I'd have slapped his face!"

"Maybe that's why he didn't kiss you," I said, quietly. It made me feel sorry for Lilie. Still, the truth is that I was rather sure he wouldn't have kissed Lilie anyway.

FIVE

Papa was behaving strangely.

We were used to his getting angry at the slightest irritation, but now he flew into a fury at nothing at all. He would ask some ordinary question and someone would answer it, then suddenly Papa's face would contort and he would scream,

"Why are you mocking me? How do you dare to laugh at me?" and he would make as if to strike the person who had answered. Not Mama, of course, nor a visitor, but one of the children, or delivery people, or such. Once he flew out at Thad, who actually that time hadn't done anything; he was going to hit Thad and Thad naturally put up his arm to shield himself, but Papa began to yell,

"Put your arm down!" and tried to hit him without Thad making any attempt to protect himself.

Now that of course can't be done; it is sheer instinct

42

to defend yourself. This little scene went on for several minutes till finally Mama looked out of the kitchen into the hall and saw it, and she called out, in a desperate tone,

"Ezekiel! what is wrong with you?"

Then Papa slammed back into another room.

Mama and Lilie had many secret discussions now, and they went about looking pale and worried. During the autumn and winter, and as spring came on, he was more and more curious in his behavior. Usually he looked neat, but now he was sometimes over particular about his appearance, and sometimes quite careless. When we disagreed with him he would say we were all his enemies! He would stand in front of the fire in our kitchen and keep sniffing the air.

"Fumes," he would mutter. "Fumes are coming up when I stand here. My enemies are trying to poison me."

Then he would refuse to eat something that Ada, the woman who sometimes came in to help Mama, had cooked for him. (He always had to have separate meals because of the unusual hours at his school, with its late afternoon and evening classes.) Mama would try to argue with him, but he insisted that someone was paying Ada to poison his food. Poor, simple, hardworking Ada! Why else, he demanded, did she come? Why, indeed! I never saw her paid anything. I think she admired Mama and pitied her, with all the children and such difficulties, and Mama would have her sit down to tea with her at the kitchen table and she'd tell Ada her troubles and then she'd sing and tell stories and jokes.

And then, poor Ada had little choice. When I first saw her I was very frightened and wanted to run away. A stove had exploded in her face, a year or two before, when she was a young, engaged girl. Now her hair was growing back, short, tousled and colorless, and you soon got used to her seared eyebrows, blistered cheeks and red-veined nose. She told everyone how she had been sure, when she was ready to leave hospital, that her young man would run away at the sight of her.

"But my Jim," she would tell us, "he just blinked his eyes a bit. Then he said, 'Well, old gal, there's a bit o' silver lining 'round every cloud. I won't have to be jealous of yer now, when I'm away!' "

One wouldn't think that a consoling remark, actually, but she knew what he meant, and under the circumstances it must have sounded like pure poetry to Ada! And they were married as if nothing had happened. Jim was a sailor and glad enough to have a little home to come back to. Ada was a small but muscular woman, kept a clean flat, and had "a bit in the bank for a rainy day," in the bargain. Jim was a

spry, thin, red-headed chap, good-natured; and he
too, when he was home between voyages, would come
in and help around; he trained the creepers from the
wall of our house across the narrow path on to the
fence that divided our garden from the neighbor's.
In spring I loved to see those little five-fingered red-
pink leaves so tenderly opening, like tiny wrinkled
hands, greening, spreading, to draw a low roof of sun-
dappled shade across the stone path.

How cruel and strange it seemed to imagine Ada
trying to kill Papa. Didn't Papa understand that it
couldn't be true? Didn't grown people *know?*

Then a doctor came to the house,—not our regular
one, who came when the children were sick. And
then a third, together with ours. Three doctors all
together. Lilie told me hastily they were for Mama,
because she was over-tired and was beginning to find
it hard to walk. But then why did Mama and Lilie
wait in the bedroom while the doctors talked to Papa
in the parlor, with the doors closed?

I remember the dark, troubled look on the face of
one of the doctors, as they came out. He saw Mama
and Lilie waiting anxiously in the hall, took off his
gold pince-nez eyeglasses and put them on again, and
pursed his lips sadly.

I was quickly pushed away.

They explained to me later, with a terrible, strange

word—and I had thought I knew all words—that wriggled into the shadows of my consciousness like an unearthly reptile trailing terror:

"Paranoia. That's what one of the doctors said."

What *was* that?

Lilie, herself pale but keeping a calmness, would have answered, but Mama said, with grim, mystified tones,

"Exaggerated ego. But the other doctors say no."

Did that mean Papa was going to be insane? I felt the house shake around me.

Eddie added, but there was more of scornfulness than fear in his voice,

"He could cure everything that's wrong with the world, only the world won't let him."

"But that isn't what the other doctors said," Mama insisted. "The old doctor said it was because Papa fell down off his bicycle and hit his head on the pavement, and now there was a bone pressing on his brain."

"The young doctor says it isn't that," Lilie argued. "Pa just had a bump from that fall. And our own doctor, he's known Papa so long, he says it's a plain ordinary nervous breakdown and he says he doesn't wonder at it, and he says what do we need all those new long words for, it's still the same thing. He says Papa needs a complete change, that's all. And we—"

46

Eddie broke in on Lilie.

"Fat lot *he* knows. The *old* chap's been a brain specialist all his life. What did Pa have to get a bicycle for, and go riding alone on Sundays in the country, except he's so selfish he wants everything good all to himself?" Eddie finished tying a bootlace with an angry jerk of his wrist. His foot didn't come off the chair by itself, at first, and he had to shove it down with his hand.

It was decided. The only real cure for Papa would be complete change of scene, and a new start.

That meant America.

The only geography we knew was that of England. It took up a whole page of our geography book. We didn't have a globe. England and her possessions, outlined or colored in red, in distant countries on back pages. We had also learned that England never lost a war. The war with America? Oh, *that* was a revolution. It was English against English.

Changes would happen to us, in London, that was sure. The father, going away . . . But I did not feel that it would be anything much worse.

Papa did not speak to us about his going.

Mama told us that he would not be all alone there. Mama's brother, who was our Uncle Mark, and his wife, Aunt Sara, lived in New York. And they knew

47

each other from before. Mama and Papa had met for the first time in New York; they had come from different parts of Russia. When they were mere teenagers, the Russian Tsarist government had issued anti-Jewish decrees that had made it almost impossible for Jews to study or earn a living in Russia. Thousands of them had emigrated, mostly to America.

Papa had become an ardent Zionist; that means, he was convinced that the only hope for the Jews to survive was to win back the land of Palestine (Zion) as a national homeland. So he never taught Hebrew to private pupils or in a school without also teaching the history of the Jews, which is in fact very interesting, full of heroes and heroines and dramatic events. Papa could make it sound absolutely fascinating. Yes, Papa could make any boy or girl feel proud to be Jewish, instead of being ashamed of it, as people of a minority often are. So he taught them to be Zionists. Many of his pupils later went to Palestine, to work as farmers or builders.

But many Jews disagreed with the whole idea. Mama hadn't seen it his way, nor had her brother, Uncle Mark. They were sure the Jews would never be able to go to Palestine. They thought it was better, and safer, for Jews to become a part of the countries they were living in, while keeping to the Hebrew faith as much as possible. Uncle Mark's wife, Sara, had also opposed Zionism, and used to make jokes about it.

Papa felt more and more unhappy in such an atmosphere. He decided he ought to join a group of Zionists who were going to Palestine to pioneer, some of them with their wives and children. But Mama would not hear of it. She told him, "If you go to Palestine, you go without me." So that settled it. Then some other friends told him it would be just as useful for him to go to London where they were forming new Zionist groups, and they thought he would find the life there more suitable.

Mama did not really want to go, but her brother had married (he used to live with them) and so she did not object. So they came to London. They liked it, but it was a hard life. Papa gave private lessons in Hebrew before he became headmaster of the school. Lilie was born and they wanted to give her a good start in life. But there was an epidemic and the baby nearly died.

They decided it had been easier to make a living in New York, and they were planning to go back. Mark had now become a dentist and was willing to lend them the money for their tickets to the United States.

But then Mama became ill. One day she suddenly fell down on her hands and knees and could not get up. The doctors agreed there was something wrong with her spinal system, but they could not decide what the trouble was, or what to do about it. She was taken to a nursing home, near London. She often talked to us about it, in later days, and told us how beautiful the garden was there, and how kind they all were to her. In a few months she had seemed to be quite well again, and she went back home to Papa and the baby.

She was very happy for a while, she used to tell us. But perhaps she really never did quite recover her health. She would get tired so quickly, and she never went out unless she had to, except around the corner for shopping.

Papa got along in London all right for years. But his expenses of course kept getting higher; we were growing up but not earning anything yet, and his first pupils were finished studying now; he was not so young any more, and it was harder to get new private pupils. And besides, he didn't seem to get along well with anybody in London, now.

So our doctor told him, "Go back to New York. That is the place for people to start again. You have a brother-in-law there; you will not be alone. Let your wife and children wait here, and when you are ready, they will come and join you."

Letters were written to America. Answers came.

It was arranged that Papa should go by himself. He would get a teaching position in New York, and when he had saved enough money, he would send us tickets to come over.

We all went to the station to say goodbye to him. There stood his two little valises beside the track; one was new. He kissed us all goodbye; he embraced Mama a long time, and kissed her. When he had gone away on the little train that went the cheapest way to Southampton, to the ship, Mama turned round to us; her eyes were red with crying.

She put her hand on Eddie's shoulder; he had grown almost as tall as she.

"You are now the man of the house," she told him.

Eddie shrank; he seemed to look paler and shorter than usual when she said that.

SIX

So Eddie left school on the day that he became fifteen. He wanted to go to work.

Mama begged him not to; he could earn so little. We were managing to live on the allowance that was being supplied to us—I never knew by whom, but it was probably the Jewish community for whom Papa had organized the school.

Every Thursday afternoon Mama sent me to the East End, to the home of "the Secretary," to collect and bring back the cash. This Secretary was a worried little man with spectacles and black hair that stood up—perhaps it was standing up at the idea of a neglected little wretch like me carrying home three gold half-sovereigns loose in my pocket through a crowded, busy commercial neighborhood! On the other hand, my appearance was probably better protection than a guard; who would imagine that I carried more than a loose ha'penny or two?

Thirty shillings a week wasn't much. I remember Mama, usually so fastidious, looking regretfully at an open paper-wrapped parcel which Ada was showing her. "I wish I *could* cook this for us," she said. I glanced at it, a little flayed body like red jelly, and I gasped, "Oh—no!" But Mama said, "It's rabbit; other people eat it. And it's only a shilling. But it isn't kosher." Mama looked annoyed about it, but I was glad. I couldn't have touched it. One day we came home and there wasn't any dinner. We ate bread and butter.

Eddie was growing too fast, Mama said.

She worried about his needing new boots, an overcoat, and such. Papa's letters came regularly, but as yet he did not send us any money. I wondered why he always addressed her as "My Beloved," but while he was here they had quarreled about almost everything.

Eddie didn't seem to worry about himself; he worried about us. He said I should have had a white dress for the school photograph at the end of last term. I could hardly be seen in the class picture, because I had to be hidden behind all the others, although I had won a city scholarship with the all-time highest grade for our borough.

Eddie said he could start school again in America, when Papa brought us over there. His first job didn't pay much, and anyway the man closed up and went off without paying anybody. Then a friend of Papa's gave him a reference and he was taken on as assistant packer in a supply house on Bond Street for ladies' imported neckwear, made in France. He earned fourteen shillings a week, and gave Mama eight.

He tried to be quite the grown-up gentleman toward Mama and Lilie and even to me. He would raise his cap when he met us outside the house; he opened doors for us. And if we were going anywhere with him, he paid our bus fare—really paid it, I mean, instead of only taking our pennies and handing them to the conductor.

Christmas time came.

Christmas always made me feel more lonely and leftout than ever. Papa had tried to make our Hanukkah holiday very pleasant, to compensate for the excitement that Christmas brought to other children. He would bring home the box of many-colored candles; we picked our colors and put them in the nine-branched candelabrum, and lighted them at night and sang Hanukkah songs. And he gave us each some "Hanukkah money," and recited the ancient Hebrew blessings over us,—that the boys should grow up to be like the patriarchs Abraham, Isaac and Jacob, and the girls like the mothers in Israel, Sarah, Rebekah, and Rachel.

I think I should tell here why our names weren't Jewish-sounding. Before Lilie was born, Papa had been trying to teach Mama to read the Bible in Hebrew, but she hadn't the patience. Only she noticed the name Lilith in the Commentary, and she liked it. Papa explained to her that Lilith was supposed to have been a "not-good one," a primitive female spirit which had an evil influence on Adam. But Mama had said there were no such creatures. Papa wanted to call the baby Jael, but Mama said Jael had killed General Sisera, so why was Jael a better name? And Papa couldn't make her see the difference. She said she just liked the sound of Lilith. So they agreed to call the baby Lilith Deborah. When Lilie grew old enough to go to school, they asked her to choose which name she liked; she picked Lilie, but wanted it spelled "Lilie" so that it would be different from just Lily. We all had second names which we never used.

For the same reason, I suppose—that we shouldn't feel Christmas brought more to Christian children than Hanukkah did to Jewish ones—it had been the custom for us to be taken to the yearly pantomime play that was performed at the Drury Lane theatre every Christmas week. Lilie would take us. Papa and Mama never went, though Mama liked the pantomime. I suppose there wasn't enough money.

We had the cheapest seats, "late doors," or unreserved, for the Family Circle. For us it was exciting even to wait in the crowded line; some people came very early and brought boxes or stools to sit on, and often street singers or jugglers came around to entertain during the tedious last hour. And oh, the rush when "late doors" opened, and the happy scamper up endless steps!

That winter, after Papa had gone away, they gave *The Sleeping Beauty*, and we were depressed at home because we couldn't go. We wouldn't see the "Transformation Scene"—the sudden changing of the castle and the forest from spring to winter, with "real" snow gently falling, and the tinsel-sparkling princess with all the royal court suddenly struck asleep just as they were, and the forest swiftly overgrowing and hiding the castle, and then at the end, everyone suddenly comes back to life! The forest swiftly changes back to springtime, and the music sounds so gay, and in the meantime we had a bag of bonbons to share, and the marvelous costumes and jewelry to wonder at!

We knew we couldn't afford all that now. We were heavy-hearted, but no one said a word.

And then, on the evening before the very last day

SYBIL

of the pantomime, Eddie came in from work and
spoke to Mama in the kitchen. And he held up before our eyes an envelope marked "Christmas Bonus."
He handed it to Lilie and said,

"You're going. Take the kids."

"Going? Where?" she said, astonished.

Mama said, proudly, "To the pantomime! Eddie
has given us his bonus!"

We all fell upon Eddie with kisses; he looked so
grown-up and happy. Then with a noble gesture he
took out of his pocket two extra shillings, saying hand-
somely,

"Here—I nearly forgot. For the bonbons."

Mama was not going, and Eddie refused to go
either; she told us later how he had stayed home and
made the lunch and the tea for her and himself, because she got tired so quickly nowadays. She told him
to go out with his friends, but he said no, she would
be all alone then.

And then began lovely surprises!

Eddie brought home his salary every two weeks, and
always counted out more than half of it into Mama's
hand. She always grieved about taking it—but it was
sixteen shillings toward the monthly rent of twenty-
five.

Then after he'd given her the money, he would
bring out a package. Mama, Lilie and I would look

57

on with fascinated delight, for he would open it and out would come the most beautiful, delicate silks and satins and velvets and laces, in exquisite colors,—a rolled, tube-like tie in violet satin, and another in pink; a triple fall of fairy-like lace; a wide fichu, two almost in the same style, and a third slightly different; a jabot of sky-blue silk, some lace yokes, once even a blousette of incredibly fine lace.

Lilie was the eldest so she chose, first for Mama, then for herself, and I got the rest.

And later, one after another, on three separate occasions, a full-length scarf of ivory-tinted lace, with a flower design, scalloped edges, and inset at each end, an oval panel; the detail was different on each scarf. The first was given to Mama; two weeks later, there was one for Lilie, and the third time it was actually for me.

But the third scarf Mama held in her hands a few moments, before she passed it to me, and there was a flicker of anxiety in her deep eyes. She said to Eddie, who was watching us proudly,

"Isn't it wonderful, how they give you all these things for us!"

Lilie was looking a bit serious. She passed her tongue over her lips several times, then pressed them together and did not say anything.

"Mama—give it to me—come on—" I exclaimed.

I was already gloating over its long and airy loveliness.
I took it across my fingertips, hovered it about my
tousled head, and held up my face, smiling. I was the
lost princess at the magic casement—indeed "o'er
perilous seas"—if we had known!

"Sybil will grow up to be a beauty!" exclaimed
Mama, happily.

"You might at least comb your hair before you put
that lace on it," crabbed Lilie, "or God forbid maybe
even wash it."

"I wanted to wash it last night but you wouldn't
get out of the bathtub," I reminded her, but cheerily
because of the loveliness that had come into my
hands.

"You do extra work for them, Eddie?" Mama ventured.

"Oh, they're leftovers. I get them instead of a
raise. They leave them in a box for me. They're things
rich ladies order and then send back."

I saw Lilie glance at the side of the box. Yes, the
name "Eddie" was scribbled on it. I thought I caught
a couple of other words after his name, but Eddie
quickly took the box away.

The wonder went on for several weeks more. We
did not suspect anything.

We had known something like it on a long-before
Hanukkah holiday, while Papa was here, when a great

basket had been delivered at our door, on the first day of the celebration.

We had sometimes received things like a pack of damp straw, and inside it a large, shiny-scaled fish— a turbot caught by one of the wealthy fathers of Papa's private pupils (there weren't many wealthy ones). Or a pair of brown-feathered birds, which Mama didn't know how to cook. Or a rather battered wooden rocking horse called Neddie, which we all adored; it had a ragged gray mane that had probably once been white.

This basket had been splendidly untouched, of shining new yellow wicker, bound in broad, smooth silk ribbons, and packed with glorious jars of imported jellies, shiny white boxes of French chocolates and cakes and tall bottles of wine with gold seals unbroken! It had been opened by Papa and Mama under the Hanukkah Menorah, when the first-night candle was lighted, and we had been allowed to choose one gift each. Papa told us later that one of his few West End pupils had persuaded his family to sacrifice their own holiday treat, and had asked Papa never to tell us who sent it!

So it seemed to me—and to Mama and Lilie too, I suppose—that these laces and silks were something of the same nature.

Then, one evening, after supper of meatballs and

mashed potatoes—Mama made them taste delicious, she could cook so well that even our perennial dessert of stewed prunes had a taste to it—the street-door bell rang.

Lilie went and opened it.

In front of her, a man walked in. He took his hat off. He was middle-aged, spare, and wore glasses. He looked straight at Eddie, without saying a word.

Eddie's oval, rather strongly straight-featured face had gone quite pale. He did not move in his chair. Now the blood began to pulse back, and deepened gradually till it was a flood of scarlet, all over his forehead and cheeks and chin, leaving just one small, hard white spot in his right cheek.

"You are Mrs. Raphel?"

Mama could only nod. Lilie's mouth was wide open.

"I wish to speak to this boy's father, madam."

"I am his mother. Speak to me."

I was a bit surprised to hear Mama answer up like that. But I had noticed that men never got really angry with her, even when they came to collect the rent and she didn't have it. She would just look at them sadly, and if there were tears in her eyes they would turn around quickly and go away. Then a letter would come and she wouldn't open it.

The man's voice softened.

"Madam, I'm afraid I must ask for an interview with his father."

"His father—is in America!" said Mama, dramatically.

"Ah!" The man pursed his lips under his little brown mustache.

"Sybil, go and see if Thad's in bed," said Mama.

I ran out willingly. I felt that there was trouble and perhaps shame for Eddie, and that it was because he had done something wrong trying to give us what we had no hope of having otherwise, something of the beauty of the rich world beyond us. And I felt he would not want me to be there while it was talked about.

Thad was asleep on his narrow cot in Eddie's room; I could see by the oblong beam of gaslight reflected from the frosted-glass window of the hall. He looked so small among the tossed blankets, so forgotten. And then I saw that our big gray cat—an ugly, stupid fellow that we had to take when our nice white cat Spot disappeared—this ugly cat was on the bed, hunched up asleep, near Thad's face! So I crawled over the bed, loose-stringed boots and all, and shoved and pushed at the cat till it leapt squealing down on the other side, in the narrow gap between the bed and the wall.

Thad turned, whimpered, but did not wake up. I

felt a pang of pity for him, and I stroked the top of his rumpled head; his small fist lifted spasmodically and caught me on the nose. It shocked me, like a miniature of the way I felt life treated us Raphels. But how be hurt at something a child unconsciously did? I couldn't help laughing at myself. I got off the bed, covered Thad closely up to his neck, then searched under the bed until I could see the cat. Then I got a broom from the hall and poked the cat out of the bedroom and shut the door so it couldn't creep in again.

I went slowly back to the kitchen. The man was leaving. At the door I heard him finishing a sentence,

"—in consideration of his youth. But I trust, young man, that you—"

He saw me, and stopped short. Then he took the hand Mama offered him, and held it.

"My gratitude," said Mama, fervently.

The man was looking into Mama's pleading eyes.

"We will wrap up the—the articles," Mama said, proudly, "He will bring them all back, tomorrow."

"On consideration—in view of the fact—after all, the articles having been out of our hands, they will no longer be saleable"—he glanced at me, now, untidy and mussed as I must have looked then—and he sighed. "We will consider that aspect of the matter—terminated. If, at any future time, the family should be in a position to compensate"—but he stopped, as if it were no use to continue.

Abruptly he let go of Mama's hand. She was trying to smile, but her mouth trembled.

"Er—goodnight. I—wish you well. And—the matter is closed." The door shut quietly behind him as he left, and Mama burst into tears.

"He is a gentleman," she sobbed, to nobody.

Eddie was sitting just as before, even his face hadn't moved, only it was very pale.

Lilie still wore her things when she went out, but I don't know what I did with mine. I don't seem to remember them, after that.

SEVEN

Eddie didn't get another job, though he went out early in the morning, and did not come back till suppertime. He hardly spoke to any of us now. I could tell he felt too ashamed, especially because Lilie and I had been there when the man from the store came up.

He explained, one evening, to Mama and me, suddenly, while she was mending socks and I was drying supper dishes.

He told us he had worked in the wrapping section of the shipping department, assistant to a white-haired man named Tyne. Mr. Tyne had seemed very kind; he took an interest in Eddie, and asked him about his family, and where he had been to school, and what he expected to do in life.

Mr. Tyne had been at the store a long time. He was allowed to bring up hot tea from the company kitchen and to drink it there in the packing-room. He would

65

take an extra cup from below the shelf and invite
Eddie to share. He kept a packet of granulated sugar,
and they used the same spoon. Eddie wasn't really
supposed to take the time out. But it was nice, on
chilly days, in that big, bare, unheated room, filled
with shelves and boxes, to pull his own stool over and
have a swallow or two of hot tea. Mr. Tyne would
talk about the unfairness of the world, and say it
wasn't right for some people to ride in fine carriages
and have all the beautiful things. And one time Eddie
saw a box that Mr. Tyne kept hidden below the shelf,
and it was full of silks and laces.

Now, when ladies came into the store and wanted
to buy, all kinds of things would be brought out to
show them, and whatever they didn't take would be
put in a box marked "return to shelf." Mr. Tyne or
Eddie were supposed to sort these out and put them
back in their proper boxes.

Well, Eddie didn't want to tell us, and we didn't
really want to know, just how it was done. But Mr.
Tyne had showed Eddie how he could get boxes of
things out of the store to bring them home, without
being noticed. Mr. Tyne said he had been doing it
for years and they never found out.

Mama began to cry when he came to that.

Then Eddie stopped explaining and got angry.

"I was just trying to get a few nice things for you

and for Lilie and Syb! You know Papa never cared how any of us looked. He never cared if we never had clothes, except sometimes when it was Rosh Hashanah and he wanted us to come to synagogue with him."

"Papa never had enough money," Mama said.

Eddie stormed on. "Remember that winter when he bunched Syb up in a rotten old blanket because her coat was all torn, and he tied a piece of *rope* around it to hold it up, and she cried and wouldn't go to school? A lot he cared how any of you looked!"

"Eddie, but the world *is* as it *is*, you can't make it better by doing wrong," Mama said, strongly. "Think, —if everybody did the same thing, where should we all *be*? And, you know, Eddie,—they might—the manager—he might have taken you to—to—" She could not make her mouth say the awful words, about our own Eddie.

Eddie hung his head and looked away. There was something deep in his frowning eyes that made me feel sure he felt as ashamed as we did. Then Mama leaned forward to him, and put her hand on his.

"Promise me, Eddie . . . *Promise* me . . .

"All right. I promise," he said, and he sounded relieved.

Mama wiped her eyes.

"If I had ever thought he would bring me into such

poverty," she muttered, bitterly. "That *my* child should . . ."

"It's over, Ma," I said, firmly.

"I'll get a different job," said Eddie.

"They'll ask you where you worked before," I worried.

"Thanks for telling me, Miss Sybil! I wouldn't have known that!" he snapped.

"I didn't mean—"

"Shut up, then."

He stamped out.

But somehow he didn't take another job. I know one of Papa's friends in London had a little chandler's shop, and wanted Eddie to help, but Eddie wouldn't.

Then Mama stopped sending me to collect the thirty shillings from the Secretary in the East End. Papa had gotten a position in New York, and every two weeks his letter contained a small blue paper. She would have to go to the post office with it and sign her name, and they would give her money. Lilie or I used to go with her after school. But sometimes the letter was late—and then Mama would cry, and worry, maybe something had happened to Papa, or the letter had been lost. It always came, after a while. Once a letter came from Uncle Mark, and it had a blue paper, too.

Eddie explained that he was trying to get a decent

job, not just packing things up or selling stuff across the counter. But he was too young to get anything responsible.

Then he was always angry. I didn't know what had become of the old Eddie, with his jokes and his kind ways, even though they were often rough. He stopped bothering about being "gentlemanly." He would still help us do things around the house that girls couldn't do, but only if *nobody* asked him to! We would put something where he would see it,—like a chair that had a pulled-out rung, or a table whose leaf wouldn't fit back, or we'd shove a chair against a wall where the paper had peeled off,—though Mama was afraid to let him climb a stepladder. And he'd repair what he could.

But if anyone *asked* him—whooh! he'd fly into a fury and ask if he was supposed to be the laborer or the housemaid. (Ada had had to leave for a regular job where she was paid, but she kept a room with us and did some work weekends, and her husband Jim was often here to help; he had a job on the river now, and did not take long trips any more.)

Lilie was at high school and then at a part-time teaching job most of the day, and I think when she came home and did her homework she was too tired to notice much what was happening with Eddie.

But he was being worse and worse at home. One

afternoon I heard him arguing with Mama. He spoke louder and louder—and then he came out and pushed past me and went out the door.

Mama was sitting there, sad and worried.

"Oh, Sybil,—I'm afraid—Eddie might try to leave home. Who knows what will become of him?"

I shook my head. "He'll never do that. He's only talking. He did a bad thing and he feels sick about it. But he didn't do it for himself. He did it because he thought it would make us happy. Now he knows he was wrong. He'll get over it. You'll see."

I gave Mama a big hug. She smiled at last.

As it turned out, I was quite right about that.

But then, Eddie's accident happened.

EIGHT

It was the beginning of the second summer that Papa
had been away. I had taken Mama over to the Post
Office that afternoon; it was a rainy sort of day, and
the wind plagued us like cold fingers poking around
our necks and wrists and ankles.

Mama came home very tired. Our doctor—he was
an old friend of Papa's and never charged us a fee—
had told her to take hot baths when she felt ex-
hausted.

She thought that a hot bath now would be good
for her. But the faucet of the tub in the bathroom,
on the second floor, was out of order, and the hot
water came through very slowly, and wasn't very hot.
Mama decided to put a big saucepan of water to boil
on the kitchen stove; two trips up to the bathroom,
each time with one pailful, would add enough hot
water to the tub.

I helped her fill the big saucepan and carry it on to the stove. Though it was June, it was still cold enough to have a good fire going.

Eddie was sitting in the kitchen, reading a blue paper-backed booklet, one of the "Gem" series of public-schoolboy adventures; he had just buttered a side of cottage loaf and was eating the thick piece of bread.

Mama should have just said, "How shall we get the hot-water pail up the stairs?" or she might have called Jim, who was out in the garden somewhere pruning the rosebush and its little hedge; Jim had planted it and was very proud of its two buds. Then Eddie would have offered to carry up the pail.

But she forgot and called Eddie.

"Eddie," she said, "can't you put down the book and carry up the hot water?"

Eddie looked up, his gray eyes with that smoky look they often had now, a sort of anger sign, and answered,

"Can't I even read quietly in this house any more?"

"All right," I said, quickly, "I'll do it."

Eddie flung the book down, with the buttered bread on top of it, and came over to the stove.

"You let it alone!" he snapped.

He splashed the water from the saucepan so jerkily into the pail that I was afraid.

"Well, let me help," I said.

"Keep out of the way! I don't need your help! Why don't you go and comb your hair, Miss Rat-tails!"

He grabbed the pail and turned and started up the stairs to the bathroom. Mama began wiping up the spilled water, while I nervously watched Eddie hastening up the narrow flight.

Eddie was nearly at the top when he turned his head as if to shout something at me—and his foot slipped.

He never made the last step.

He came tumbling backward down the whole flight of stairs, the scalding water sloshing all over his right side. Mama jumped up, wringing her hands and screaming, "God oh God oh God—" like one word.

Jim rushed in from the garden; he was just about coming in anyway, and was close enough to seize Eddie's shoulders and keep his head from hitting the ground.

I rushed outside, not quite knowing why. I ran in at the nearest gate, banged on the door, and when the startled woman opened it, I squealed,

"A doctor! A doctor!"

A young man ran out, saw me, instantly put on his

coat and ran up the street to where another doctor, not ours, lived.

Three weeks later, Eddie came back from the hospital. He was thinner and white-faced; he still had huge blisters all over his right thigh and his right leg.

He had to sit in a wheelchair, and would have to for another few weeks, the doctor said.

But this was not the terrible part.

We didn't know *that* yet.

The blisters healed at last. Eddie was much nicer to all of us again, and when the doctor came for the last time, to send the wheelchair back and give him a few final instructions, everyone was relieved.

But, strangely, the doctor did not look so. And, oddly, he took Mama aside, and asked her questions, not about Eddie, but about herself. And when he left, his face was quite grim and sad. He shook hands with Mama and Ed and they thanked him for his care; then he suddenly turned to me:

"Are you the one who was by—you *saw* your brother fall?"

"Yes—" I stammered, surprised.

"Was his left foot *on* the step?"

"Yes—"

"And his right foot—was it *on* the step—did it slip off *after* he had put it on the step?"

"No—I—I think—it didn't really come up on to the step—it sort of tried to but it didn't—"

"Aha!" The doctor nodded sharply, as if my answer had told him more. Then he went away.

Finally, in the spring of the next year, THE letter arrived from New York.

We were all to leave for America in four weeks. Papa had sent us the tickets. Some of the money he had borrowed, but most of it he had saved. We were going steerage, of course, like most immigrants, rather more like baggage than people. But we had no choice; there the tickets were.

I wasn't sure if I was glad, but like all of us, I was excited.

Eddie was tremendously relieved. In New York, he was certain, he would be able to get the kind of job he wanted. He felt confident and eager.

Lilie wondered if the young men were different over there. She hoped so.

Mama was joyful. She would see her beloved brother Mark again,—after twenty years of thinking they would never meet again. Uncle Mark was doing well, and he had written her. He and Aunt Sara had found an apartment for us, and were helping Papa buy furniture.

People congratulated us. We would make money in
New York. Everybody got rich in America.
The sun had risen—in the west!

NINE

"Oh, America's beautiful. I love it!"

"Listen to her! In five minutes, she knows!"

You could almost guess it was me saying the first, and Lilie snipping me off with the second!

I couldn't blame Lilie, though. We were just coming up out of the subway at One Hundred and Tenth Street and Lenox Avenue. I was flying ahead while she was keeping a grip on Thad up the stairway and trying to help Mama, too. Papa and Eddie were carrying baggage.

We had had ten days on the dreadful ship; the weather that March had been stormy, the cabin smelly and suffocating, the food miserable. We had all been seasick except Lilie and Mama; they probably had had no time to be sick!

But now we were free! The spring air was crisp and bright, with a thrust of new life in every breath. The sky seemed far more high and more blue than over London; sunlight was everywhere, the park alongside was waving masses of fresh little green leaves, as though to welcome us in. I felt it was going to be springtime now, forever and ever.

Papa had met us at the ship, after we went through a very large room with a long wooden rail. He looked as usual, so our own doctor had been right after all, it *was* just a nervous upset that he had had. He was his old self really, only his beard was shorter and more pointed. He didn't look specially happy to see us, and though it seemed more natural to be having Papa with the rest of us again, I don't think I felt any joy about it. He kissed us all quickly, then embraced Mama and Lilie. I didn't like the way he looked at Eddie, and Eddie turned his head away at first. I suppose Mama had written something about Eddie giving trouble, though I don't think she really explained how.

But there was another man who came up to us quickly. He was shortish, but handsome, and he smiled pleasantly at us all. He had soft wavy black hair and deep brown eyes like Mama; we could see he was Mama's brother. Mama ran up to him with a cry, and they kissed each other many times; there were tears in her eyes, but she smiled as she wiped them away.

"I'm Uncle Mark," he said to us, kindly; he kissed Lilie and me, and shook hands with the boys, even

Thad, who had marched up to him and was looking him over with curiosity, twisting a bit of his hair as he usually did when he felt puzzled. Thad was nearly eight, then.

There was a lot of talking and then we went into the subway, to go to Uncle Mark's house and meet Aunt Sara and their little girl, Claire.

People here lived in apartments, not separate little houses; the streets were very short, the houses tall and square and all-in-one, no gardens, nothing in front but a few steps and then a door.

Papa and Uncle Mark had to walk rather slowly because Mama could not keep up with them unless they did. Uncle Mark noticed this, and I heard him say to her,

"Is this what you meant, in your last letter? that you were not as lively as you used to be? Of course, twenty years have passed—but you were always light on your feet—you haven't become much heavier that I can see, but you do move much more slowly."

Mama did not say anything. Uncle Mark went on,

"Is it—do you think it might be—something for which you would need to see a doctor?"

"I don't know, Mark," she sighed.

"We'll have to wait and see, I suppose. If you don't improve, I can find you a doctor who will see you. You must not neglect this." Just then he glanced at

Eddie, and a startled look came into his eyes. He must have noticed that Eddie walked with a slight limp.

"Eddie had an accident," Mama explained. Uncle Mark looked relieved.

"Oh, that explains it. It looked almost like a family thing."

We turned right of the park and then went up another street. Here was Uncle Mark's house. It was nice white stone; the steps were clean and some brass plates on the side of the door were neat and polished. One had his name on it, Dr. Mark Brenner, D.D.S. We went up steps; Mama almost missed one, but Papa grabbed her arm. Eddie almost missed it, too. Uncle looked again at both of them, but he said nothing.

Uncle Mark put his key in the door but a maid came and opened it before the lock turned. She wore a white cap and a white apron, and I gazed in astonishment: she was all black all over, a beautiful bright black, smooth and with a glow that was almost purplish, like ripe plums. I had never seen such a lovely dark color. I was just going to say so, but I remembered that Mama, who had been in America with Uncle Mark before her marriage, had told us there were people here who were black, but that it was considered very impolite to mention it to them.

80

The face was strange, but beautiful too, though she was rather old. She spoke differently from ordinary people, and her voice had no edges.

"Oh, Doctor. I'll call Miss'es."

"Are there any patients in the waiting room, Lou?"

"No, suh; it's lunchtime."

In two minutes our Thad was running around the living room, climbing up on the soft chairs, pulling at the heavy white curtains with their wide borders of lace, with Lilie dragging him off and making him sit down. But Lou smiled at him.

"Don't yo' be a little wild Indian, now," she warned. "Sit nice and wait fo' yo' lunch."

We waited in the living room. Lilie's eyes were looking green with nervousness.

Aunt Sara marched in at last. We recognized her from photographs Uncle Mark had sent us in London, of a smooth-faced, large, blondish woman, smiling smugly as she held a young baby, cheek to cheek; on the other side of this pair of photos the baby, then about a year old, was leaning back in her arms and pinching its mother's cheek with its hand, the way babies do, and Aunt Sara was smiling more. Another photo showed her full-length, standing very straight, her shirtwaist buttoned all the way up to her chin, and her right hand, closed like a fist, set firmly on the polished table. That was the one Papa used to call

81

"the Commander in Chief," and we soon found out why.

"Thank goodness," said Aunt Sara, loudly, fixing her gray eyes on Lilie. "From the photo you sent your father I was afraid you were the ugliest girl in the world." She went up and kissed her. "How old are you,—seventeen? Eighteen? You'll stop wearing your hair in those coronet braids around your head. It makes you look thirty."

Uncle Mark interposed. "Let us have lunch now."

Aunt Sara greeted Mama with a faint kiss that barely touched her cheek. "So you're back in New York, Bella. What did I tell you twenty years ago? In America, even *your* husband will make a living. —Lou!"

"Ma'am?" Lou sang out from another room.

"Serve lunch."

So we trailed into the dining room, a handsome room where a central lamp of many-colored glass hung like a great strange flower from the ceiling over the long table set with a lovely crisp white cloth. Aunt Sara went on,

"What kept you so long? It's nearly two o'clock."

"There was customs," said Uncle Mark, "papers, health checking—" He stood at the armchair, waiting.

Papa and Eddie had been out in the hall, talking. Papa was looking grim, Eddie's head was drooped. We all sat down, Mama and Lilie next to Uncle Mark, who didn't take his seat till he had helped them into theirs,—Papa next to Aunt Sara who had taken the armchair at the other end; the rest of us sort of squeezed in on a bench and some other chairs. The chair on Aunt Sara's other side was not taken.

Aunt Sara called out, "Claire!" and again, "Claire!" Then a little girl in spotless blue-check gingham, her rich dark hair shining around her snowy face, and tied with an airy blue ribbon at one side, came in and sat down by Aunt Sara. Uncle Mark looked at her fondly.

"Well?" he said.

She got up with a little smile and went over and kissed him. "Good afternoon, Papa," she said. He held her tight for a few moments and then she went back to her seat. Somehow I felt afraid of her, though she was only seven. Her face was as perfect as a new coin. She was as dainty as I was not.

I couldn't resist stroking the starched whiteness of the tablecloth near my flower-sprayed plate, and passing my finger over the thick, high, white embroidery.

Lou came through the swinging door carrying a large china platter that matched the plates, heaped high with fluffy omelette. Then she brought in a bowl of green peas and a platter of hashed brown potatoes.

Uncle Mark sat looking at Aunt Sara.

"How could I tell what they'd like?" she exclaimed, defensively. "Omelette everybody eats. Ezekiel told me he still eats kosher. Our butcher doesn't have kosher steak. What do you think they had on the ship? A baked potato in its jacket and a mug of muddy water they'd get for lunch."

Everything was delicious, including the brown bread and the cinnamon cake with coffee that Lou brought in later.

Claire was making a face over the cake. "I'm glad people don't come from England every day."

"People?" Uncle Mark reproved. "It's your Aunt Bella, your Uncle Ezekiel's wife, and your cousins."

"You haven't told me their names."

Uncle Mark named us, one by one; we grinned, and at the end Claire said one "Hello" to all.

"That's some mess they made of the living room, Lou," said Claire as Lou served her a glass of milk. "You'll have to clean it all over again."

"Hush yo' mouth, now," said Lou. "Didn't yo' Daddy just tell yo' somethin'?" Lou's voice had a sound in it that was indescribable to me until I came to know more colored people, then I would say it had a sound of singing.

"Mama," Thad burst out, crunching his cake, "are we going to live *here?*"

Claire sniggered.

"Here, in New York," said Mama. "But not *here*."

"Ezekiel stayed with us two months," said Aunt Sara, "when he first came to New York last year. He wanted to eat kosher. I told him we didn't keep kosher." She smiled fatly. "We had meat cakes one day, fried. He asked if they were kosher, I said yes. He ate some, then he said, 'They're fried in butter. How could you tell me they're kosher?' 'Kosher meat and kosher butter,' I told him."

Papa turned red, and Aunt Sara laughed. "So he got mad and moved out." She shrugged her large shoulders. "Nobody cried."

Claire sniggered again.

"He could have seen it all the time," added Aunt Sara. "We always had milk on the table with our meat dinners, and butter too. I don't hold with that nonsense. Three thousand years ago, in a sub-tropical country, those decrees made sense. But today, in America, in our urban culture—!"

Papa sat quietly at the table, his lips compressed, but obviously vexed. There came into my recollection all at once a curious scene,—something that had happened years ago, a Sabbath night, in London . . . a narrow hall, outside the bedroom where Lilie and I slept. Our door was open, and I noticed—Lilie also

—that the gas jet flaring on the wall outside was burning much higher than was needed . . . soon the meter would require another shilling fed into the slot, otherwise the light would slowly dwindle and then go out, and we would be in the dark all through the house. But no observant Jew might touch a light to turn it on or off or down, once Sabbath had begun. What to do? Either it must be turned down, or a shilling must be put in, which was also forbidden on Sabbath . . . Then I saw a figure moving silently into the hall, a hand slowly reached up, took hold of the gas key, and turned the light very low. Then the shadowy figure stole away. It was Papa. And I remembered thinking, "*Papa* broke the Sabbath!" And then, "But he *had* to do one or the other." Next day, I dared to ask him . . . I was afraid he'd be angry with me. But he wasn't. He just said, quietly, "In an extremity, the Hebrew law permits a solution." I didn't know what the word extremity meant, but I understood the idea.

I felt sorry now for Papa, sitting there beside Aunt Sara, knowing it was useless to explain to her; she wouldn't want to understand.

"What can Ezekiel do?" Uncle Mark put in. "He teaches religion and religious observance. He has to keep up the pretense."

"He's not pretending. That's the trouble," Aunt

86

Sara replied. She smiled blandly, her elbows on the table, looking about her as if for applause.

Mama hadn't said a word. I knew she felt the same as Aunt Sara and Uncle Mark about religious observances, but she always tried to keep to the rules, if only for the sake of not having arguments with Papa.

"So you like this apartment, Bella?" Aunt Sara was saying.

"Oh, yes," Mama answered, "It's so much easier when one doesn't have to climb stairs. I hope ours is like this."

"You think your Ezekiel would take a good apartment?" she scoffed. "I found you an apartment, eight rooms, a clean house, light, and with electricity,—but would he take it? He wouldn't."

"He wouldn't?" exclaimed Uncle Mark, startled. "I thought he took it! Thirty dollars a month rent,— after all, it's not dear, even for him!"

"Wait, you'll see what he took," said Aunt Sara, her words broken with picking her teeth. "Your husband's position—did he tell you he's getting twenty-three dollars a week salary? That's your holy men for you. The Law commands the community to educate the children of the poor. But it doesn't command them to give the teachers a decent salary. Founding a religious school, paying its headmaster like a sweatshop factory worker. The janitor gets more."

"We'll go now," said Papa, getting up.

Aunt Sara rose. "You'll come Friday night for dinner; Lou knows a kosher butcher."

"Sara can do it right when she wants to," added Uncle Mark. "And she had better want to!"

TEN

We ran up the iron stoop together, as well as we could, pushing through children that seemed lodged on the steps, through a small-paned wooden door and up one flight of stairs, as instructed.

Eddie got in first. He looked around.

I thought he hadn't opened the door yet; the room was as dark as the hall. It was in fact fairly large, but had only one small window at the rear, over a tangled-looking fire escape; at the other side it opened into what seemed to be a kitchen, with the vista of another small room behind; we later found that the family bathroom was in back of this kitchen, like a long, narrow closet with one tiny window. To our right, this central room opened, doorless, as we now found, upon two windowless small rooms, one after another, then a room with one dark window over a two-foot wide space against a sunless wall, then into a larger room which boasted two windows over the avenue. Here another fire escape broke up the air and whatever might be called a view.

"There must have been a contest," Eddie said, "for the worst apartment vacant."

"And Pa won it," I said, bitterly.

Lilie walked about the place, her head held up in an attitude of resigned acceptance, sniffing at the varnish.

"Then he advertised for the ugliest, stiffest chairs in New York." There was a set of chairs around a dining-table, all of light, new brown, scrabbled with a few curling lines on each top.

My heart kept dropping, as if down one flight of disappointment after another. Surely this wasn't where we had to *live*. Surely it was a mistake, it would be corrected. Mama came in, stood a moment, with a despairing gaze all around—then sat down and pulled the pins out of her hat. No—I still hoped, no—

But Papa marched in, with a boy carrying a bag of groceries. In the kitchen, Lilie, still wearing her hat, lighted the gas jet over the sink, picked up the tinny new kettle from its hook, and turning on the tap, waited for the water to run fresh. The boy began to put the bag of groceries down on a chair, I seized his arm for a moment to stop him, as if then we would all run out and find another place. But he impatiently put the bag down. And that settled everything in my mind.

Yes. This was the Raphel home.

"Well," said Lilie, as we undressed to go to bed that night—we always slept in a double bed, and Lilie picked the small room past the kitchen for ours—"we can be thankful for one thing; he didn't drag us into the East Side. Ma says that's much worse."

"Worse? How, worse?"

Lilie shook out her dress and fitted it on a hanger, then set the hanger over a nail driven into the other wall.

"I'm going to get a curtain to hang over this wall; it'll be a kind of closet then." She put her underthings on the only chair, pulled in from the kitchen.

"Why did you pick this room for us? The inside room before the front room has a closet."

"Pa and Ma have to have that one, otherwise Pa'll take the front room, and that'll mean we can't ever have any friends up here. Besides, this is nearest the bathroom; we can get in mornings before Eddie and Thad."

Lilie, in her nightgown, began violently attacking her shiny waves of chestnut hair with a stiff-bristled hairbrush. She tossed her hair this way and that, over her sparkling green-gray eyes and large, soft-profiled nose.

"You brush that hair as if you were killing it," I said. "You always do everything the hardest way. You seem to think if you just do something *hard*, it's going to be right."

"Get a nightgown out of that valise."

"I'm sick of wearing your old things. They don't fit me. Your nightgowns are too long for me."

"It won't kill you, one night. I'll shorten it for you tomorrow."

The gown fell all around my feet, but it looked rather luxurious that way, I thought. As she got into bed, Lilie said, "At least we're near the park."

"There is no high school on West 114th Street," said Aunt Sara, scornfully.

"But then," I replied, in distress, "why did you tell me there was? I walked, and walked, and walked."

Aunt Sara was having her lunch.

"You were walking *west?*"

"Of course."

"There is no high school for you, not there nor anywhere."

"What *do* you mean?" I asked, impatiently.

"Either you did not see the school when you passed it, or you got tired of looking, so you come and tell

me there is no high school there. A real Raphel."
She finished her dessert and drank her coffee. "Tell
me, did you have lunch?"

"Yes, before I came." I hadn't, and she probably
knew I hadn't. But I would starve rather than admit it.

"Lou! Give her a glass of milk."

I felt I could with honor drink milk, and eat with it
the good, thick, homemade cookies Lou put on the
saucer.

An idea struck me.

"Was *that* a school—the big building with the two
wide terraces, and with towers,—like a castle?"

"That was a school," said Aunt Sara. "It was Wal-
lace High School for Girls. You will go back again
tomorrow and register before you are too late and they
tell you to wait till the fall term."

I reached the school next try. It was imposing,
almost new, constructed in a style which was partly
English Tudor and partly Walter Scott-romantic. The
girls going in and out were mostly well-dressed, and
looked politely bored with school; they wore their hair
up and did everything to appear older than possible.
Some were even made up—with powder on their
noses! Their hair-do was made larger with rolls of
artificial hair stuck inside, and their skirts were almost
as long as grownups, lower than their calves.

I was placed in a class with girls two years older

93

than I. Being the "baby" of the class, and very bright, I was made a great fuss of,—spoiled, in fact! The girls would gather round me after class to "tell me all about the United States." They treated me to desserts and candy—Lilie and I received seven cents a day each for lunch. I was astonished at the amount of money these girls had to spend! They gave me all the extras —pencils and notebooks and so forth, and tickets to the school affairs, which I rarely condescended to go to—and I never realized that they were paying for me! They would ask me to pronounce words "the English way," and would laugh with delight over my broad "a", my careful grammar and precise "-ings" and "-eds" and "ly-s," and the fact that I loved history and understood English poetry better than the teacher.

They came to me after school for help with their essays, or their Latin, or French, and were surprised that I would rather give an hour to helping them learn it than five minutes to "just writing it down" correctly for them. I was given gifts—embroidered white silk gloves, a sandalwood fan, a mosaic box, pretty painted cards.

Yes, school was fun for me,—but for poor Lilie it was another story. She had to go to high school a year because she could not enter college without a diploma, and she was older than the others. But she made two or three friends there, and impressed the teachers with her work.

I couldn't ask the girls to *my* home, even after some of them invited me to theirs. They were mostly girls of old Dutch or English families, living in the Victorian brownstone private houses that lined the neighboring streets in rows, or daughters of newly rich businessmen who dwelled in the luxury apartment buildings, then rising on Riverside Drive, six stories high, with palatial lobbies, spacious elevators, and uniformed attendants.

But there were a few, like me, children of immigrants—Italians, Jews, Bohemians, Russians, Rumanians. These looked up to me, because I spoke pure English and knew so much more than they did; was not my father a teacher? Their loving, proud glances when I answered well in class and surpassed all the "stylish" girls (who didn't care), soothed my pride, so often hurt by the snobs among the others.

Yet even the snobs were not so very bad.

One of them, "crême de la crême," descended, it was said, from the Nathan Hale family, brought for class reading a magazine with a poem about immigrants. It was called "Scum of the Earth." But the title was ironical. It was really a plea for tolerance, and it had the lines,

> Children in whose frail arms shall rest
> Prophets and singers and saints of the west.

Our teacher, looking at the immigrant girls (they usually sat together), said, *"That* means *you."*

ELEVEN

We had been in New York more than six months, and still felt a-tiptoe for some wonderful change that was to happen to us. Mama seemed now to be always warily probing Papa about a letter. Sometimes she anxiously asked one of us, "Go and see if there's a letter for Papa in the mailbox." We would tumble down the stairway, pull ajar the box, which was never locked, shout up "No," then run out to play in the street or the park.

At last one day Mama lost patience and I heard her say to Papa,

"Why do *you* not write to *him?*"

Papa blew up.

Finally Lilie told me. Papa was going to get a much better position; we would all live well. Eddie would not have to work, he would go to high school. She

97

would be able to finish high school and go to college without having to become a Hebrew teacher part-time. I'd be able to go on with high school without worrying—"but you're doing that anyhow," she threw in. "*I'm* the one that's got to worry."

"What do you expect me to do?" I protested. "Pa's making me take a part-time job at some Jewish organization office as soon as I'm fifteen. I'll believe that when I see it."

"When is all this going to happen, Papa's new position? Is it true?" I was deeply skeptical. But, still, this was America, the golden land . . .

We were walking to high school together, I for once having got up as early as Lilie. She was usually off long before me; Mama had accustomed her from babyhood to getting up early, taking a bath—nowadays she took a cold shower—and being served a hearty breakfast by Mama, then going off in plenty of time, neat and fresh. Unquestionably Lilie was The Child; the rest of us were unavoidable accumulations. But the poor girl paid a sad price for it; all the burdens, all the insoluble problems, were confided to her.

A gilded dream hung over the household now, and it was verified. A letter—THE letter—came. It bore an English crest,—an earl's coronet, no less! So Mama knew, before she put it at Papa's breakfast plate.

I ran home at lunch time. Mama and Papa were

98

screaming at each other. The letter had been opened.
Mama was saying, "Go to him! Go to his office!"

"You are wrong! You are wrong! They must come
to me! Otherwise I am merely another petitioner waiting in line!"

"Come to *this* house?" asked Mama, bitterly.

Papa set his lips, and went off to his school.

"Let me see the letter, Mama," I asked. I put on
the kettle and we had a cup of tea on the kitchen
table, and I read it. I knew the name of the Earl; I
knew that he was a noted amateur of Hebraics. He
had considered Papa a great scholar and a brilliant
teacher. In London he had helped Papa to present
himself as a very promising candidate for the new
Chair in Hebraics at the University. But for some
reason it had not gone through. Now he informed
Papa that he had written to a famous Jewish patron
of education in America, a close friend of his, request-
ing him to find an "appropriate and remunerative"
position for Mr. Ezekiel Raphel.

It was as good as done. The patron was a multi-
millionaire, generous, wise, highly respected, and his
word was law among the Jewish organizations.

"Something good *is* going to happen, Mama," I
assured her.

"You don't know Papa," she muttered. "He is in
love with his poverty!"

Papa did not write, and he did not go. And lo and behold, one morning emissaries came to Papa.

Two well-dressed gentlemen, in beautiful smooth-fitting gray suits, with gold watch chains and polished shoes, and the whitest of sharp-creased handkerchiefs showing above the breast pockets, stood at the door. There was a long conversation with Papa in the closed dining room.

Nothing came of it.

"What happened? what happened?" I demanded of Mama, as she went dark-faced and grim about the kitchen that day.

"Ask your father!" she answered between her teeth.

I had never known Mama like that. I actually went to Papa and asked him, as he sat at the table after returning from his school that night.

To my surprise, he actually answered me.

"The great patron offers to buy me out. He is opposed to everything that I have cherished and worked for, my life long. Now he offers me a huge stipend to give up Zionism, give up this my school, and to co-operate in founding a new type of religious school which to me is neither religious nor Zionistic." His deep-set blue eyes flashed at me.

"Tell me," he challenged, "would *you* accept?"

His eyes grew softer as he saw my feelings. I was trying to imagine: what if someone offered me every-

100

thing I longed for, a pleasant home, good clothes, the country, all the books I could read, luxuries even, pretty shoes, chocolates, all—if in return I would give up my hopes of honor and fame and self-respect, and live just for . . . *things.*

I knew I couldn't.

"You see," Papa said, and for once his voice was as gentle to me as if I were one of his favorite school-children. He went on, "These immigrant Jewish children here need my school. Where will they learn the Hebrew law, its eternal human ideals? Where will they learn the glory of our ancient history, to give them self-respect and pride? When we have a national homeland in our ancient country—"

But Mama stood at the door, a saucepan in one hand, a dishcloth in the other, and a bitter cry on her lips:

"*Your* children will run about in rags!"

TWELVE

When I came straight home from school one week day and found Eddie waiting about the door of our flat, I guessed he must be wanting to say something to Papa, though I could not imagine what. We used to try to be out of the house until we were sure Papa had gone to his school. And Eddie was hardly ever home; he looked for a job, or played baseball.

"Where's Mama?" I asked. That was our usual "hello" because we never felt we were home until we had seen her black upswept curly hair—she always combed it like that no matter how styles changed—and her dark eyes' relief that each was back from she knew not where. Mama hardly went anywhere now; she was always tired, and she moved heavily.

"In the kitchen," said Eddie. "Pa's still having lunch."

I went into the front room and started reading.

When I heard Eddie going down the hallway to the kitchen, I followed a few minutes later. Eddie was saying,

"—the chap I met at the Culture Club. You know. Bob."

"I know," said Pa's voice. "The one who keeps promising to get you a job at the newspaper. An excuse for you to waste your time going there instead of seeking employment."

"He *is* going to," Eddie protested. "They change off all the time. It's got to be something that I can do—"

"You can do nothing," said Pa, roughly.

Now I saw Eddie, standing near Papa, while Mama, sitting at the table, handed some dishes to Thad, who then carried them to the sink and put them under the tap.

"Don't turn on the water," I told Thad, quickly. "They've got to be scraped off first." I began doing it with a knife.

Papa slapped the table.

"That's a meat knife! These are milk dishes!"

I put the knife back on the sinkboard and took from the drawer a knife belonging to the set used for dairy food.

"You are just like your mother. Kosher means nothing to you," he muttered, angrily.

"And you think God is watching, up there," exclaimed Mama. "There are more important matters for Him."

"You have no idea of the *meaning* of it all!"

"Pa,—this fellow—Bob—"

"Yes? about the concert? You are expecting *me* to—"

"Look—the *Daily Mail* is arranging the concert for its readers. It's going to be at Carnegie Hall—and it'll only cost a dollar a seat—Beethoven's *Third* and *Ninth!*"

"Ah!" Mama's eyes glowed. "Imagine! A real concert, Eddie, with orchestra?"

"Yes—the Philharmonic Orchestra!"

"What's the bargain?" Papa demanded. "You can always get seats in the top gallery for fifty cents! So?"

"Oh—but this time it's *anywhere* for a dollar—first come first served—boxes or orchestra—one dollar. *Mama* could go because she wouldn't have to walk upstairs."

Papa, having finished his glass of tea, held it out to me for another filling. "And *you* can go at *my* expense. Is that your idea?"

"I'll have to put on more water to boil," I said.

He got up, annoyed.

"Never enough water for a second glass! I have no more time. Where is my coat?"

104

"I'll get it," I said, to keep him there a minute longer while Eddie worked on him. That concert would mean the world to Mama.

I was purposely slow getting to the big bedroom and finding Papa's coat and bringing it back. Papa was spreading two single dollar bills out flat on the table.

"Pa!"I exclaimed. "Lilie or I will have to go, too. Mama—if she—she needs help."

"Eddie will help her into the hall. They will have orchestra seats, won't they?"

"Pa!" I exclaimed again. "But she may need one of us girls!"

Papa looked irritated. But he opened his wallet, and fished out another dollar.

"*I* want to go," Thad began.

"Shut up," said Eddie, threateningly. "You don't even know what a concert is."

"Sure, that's why I—"

"Shut up!" Thad shut up, rebellious but quashed.

The only time I had been to Carnegie Hall was on a rare Saturday afternoon to a "popular," when I got into the top gallery with some school friend or other, for fifty cents. I didn't mind being high up; it was even more exciting to me, the bustling crowd, the chatter, the criticisms. But it was fascinating to think of the orchestra, or boxes even, for *us*.

Lilie wanted to be the one to go with Ma and Eddie.

105

That put me out of it. She was making a tiny salary, monitoring—you couldn't really call it teaching, she didn't know enough Hebrew yet—at Papa's school on Sunday mornings. She did offer to pay for her own ticket, so that I could go. But Eddie's friend on the newspaper was only allowed to buy four; he was giving one to his father and letting Eddie take the other three; he didn't want to go himself.

So the great evening came. I felt cruelly left out. But—somebody had to be home with Thad, after all; goodness knows what mischief he might do, left by himself, and I for one wouldn't have blamed him.

Lilie and I—it was mostly Lilie—were paying for a phonograph, in installments of five dollars a month; a costly luxury for us, but Mama loved the music so much, and soon we all felt that we couldn't live without it. Those marvelous voices were straight out of dream country for me, and even Thad would go about chanting out-of-tune the marching magic of the overture to *Rienzi* or the *Aida* ballet music, while I died over "O terr' addio!"

I put on some records for Thad, gave him supper, did my homework, and read. About ten o'clock Papa came home; I made him an omelet, with cottage cheese and black bread; he read his Yiddish newspaper, and retired to his bedroom. I made Thad wash and undress—he sometimes didn't undress unless one of

106

us made him, though he was nine years old—and he went to bed.

It was eleven o'clock and I had begun to be a bit concerned about the others; the concert was supposed to be over at ten-thirty. Still, getting out of Carnegie Hall, onto a bus, coming uptown to Lenox Avenue, —they could hardly do it before eleven-thirty.

But eleven-thirty passed, and the hand was getting too near to twelve. I was sure nothing had happened. Still . . .

The doorbell rang. I raced downstairs. They were all sitting on the steps outside, Mama, Eddie, and Lilie. A strange man stood near.

I called out, "Mama—are you all right? It's cold! Let's get in."

Eddie put his arm under Mama's shoulder, but he staggered and could not hold her up. The stranger, who had been watching, instantly ran up and seized her around her back. He was a strong, heavy, middle-aged man, and he brought her to her feet in a moment.

"Oh, thanks!" Lilie exclaimed.

"We'll manage now," said Eddie.

"Get Papa," said Lilie.

"He's in bed long ago; he'd have to get dressed," I explained. "What happened?"

"Mama couldn't get down off the bus step," said

Lilie, with a sigh. "This gentleman helped us home."

"I'm all right!" Mama exclaimed. And indeed, in the faint street light, she looked quite happy. "Just a slip of the foot. Come on, children!"

"You sure you can make it?" the man asked. "Something's wrong with that young feller, too," he added, curiously. "I'll get you up your steps—"

"It's just one flight; thank you very much," Lilie answered.

"O.K. Up to you," muttered the man. He watched a while, holding the lobby-door open, his arm ready to catch Mama if she slipped again. But we got her into the flat without too much difficulty.

"Better get a wheelchair," he called after us. It was friendly enough,—but it hit me hard.

Mama was radiant as she sat down and I made tea for us all. She was shining with the delight of the music.

I was cutting and buttering bread, and Eddie got the cheese and milk and a paper of olives out of the icebox.

"They're Papa's olives," Lilie said, a bit anxiously.

"Never mind! we will get more tomorrow," said Mama, laying her hat and scarf on a chair. She broke into singing as I put the hot tea with milk on the table before her. "Freide shane getterfunken Tochter ois Elysium"—

"Mama," I laughed, "that's Yiddish, not German!"

"So what?" said Eddie. "It's the singing that counts."

"Freude schöne Götterfunken—" I began, Eddie interrupted.

"Oh, stop showing off. So you're taking German at high school, and it's eighth term curriculum. So now we know you're good at languages. Pass the olives."

"She's the perfectionist," sneered Lilie. "Soon she'll tell us Ma's singing in the wrong key."

"Oh, children, for goodness sake, can't you talk without quarrelling? It was so happy before you began!"

I felt guilty at Ma's pained tone. It wasn't often, now that Mama laughed and sang the way she used to in London.

We heard steps coming down the hall, and we all fell quiet. Papa stood at the kitchen entrance, a wrap over his pajamas and worn slippers on his feet.

I got up and gave him my chair, but he wanted his corner chair opposite Mama. Lilie got up, gave him the corner, and took my place. I put on some more water to boil.

"Well," Pa asked, settling down, "How was the concert?"

Mama broke into smiles; her dark eyes were lovely, like sun-sparkles on deep waters. She burst into sing-

109

ing again, but substituting la-la-la for the words.

Papa was looking almost cheerful. He bit into an olive, and smiled.

"So, it was not wasted. After all, three dollars. Three—whole—dollars. Three—hundred—whole—pennies!"

"Oh, by the way—good news!" exclaimed Mama. "Eddie—tell him!"

"I got a job," said Eddie, munching black bread and farmer cheese.

"You did, Eddie?" I cried out.

"At the concert?" Pa screwed up his face suspiciously.

"That chap Bob from the Culture Club—I told you—the one who works at the *Daily Mail*—his father was there. He said the copyboy in Bob's department had quit suddenly; they need someone *pronto*. So Bob told them I'd be down there tomorrow morning at eight-thirty. And Mr. Binns said great. It's—eight dollars a week to start."

Papa hadn't a word to say.

THIRTEEN

"I'm not going," said Eddie, with finality.

It was Sunday morning and Papa wanted him to attend one of the religion classes at his school.

"Well?" Papa stood at the door, his stocky, blue-serge back, half-turned, staring anxiously at Eddie. Eddie stubbornly went on brushing and parting his brown hair, which he had wetted to pacify some insistent curling at the ends—would this were my case, I thought, watching him. My hair was so dark and straight.

"What am I to say this time?" Papa exclaimed, trying to keep his voice amiable. "The Board of Directors is to be there; they are testing my discipline. And where is my elder son?"

"I don't see what it's got to do with me." Eddie was now adjusting the knot of his green tie.

111

"If I cannot control my own children—!" Papa
stamped his foot in disgust, and I exclaimed,
"*I'll* come."

"You are a *girl!*" he muttered, vexedly.

I didn't really want to go. I had seen the school for
a few minutes, once or twice, when Mama had sent
me with a message. It was noisy there, small, untidy,
dusty, with boys rushing and pushing and shouting
as they slammed in and out of the building.

Yet there was something about seeing Papa wanting
us to come with him, hesitating to go without us, that
moved me, even though it wasn't I who he wanted.
But then he marched off, banging the door behind
him.

"I know why he wants me to go," Eddie burst out,
hotly. "It's just to make *him* look all right, good father
and all that. Make me learn to stick a cap on the back
of my head wherever I am, and get ready to go out to
a desert country digging water holes and getting shot
at by Arabs."

"You could go with him once, when the Board of
Directors are there. Maybe they'll give him a raise,
when they see he has children."

"That's the worst of it. Got to be respectful to those
penny-squeezers! They wouldn't give a raise to the
angel Elijah—"

"He wasn't an angel, he was a prophet—"

"They think they're being religious with their school, so they can sweat their factory workers and still feel safe with God! What do you mean, go there *once*. I've been to the school. I met that Nat Breit that Pa thinks is such a genius. Of all the snivelling softies! So he knows the Torah backwards and forwards. Pa wants me to be friends with *that* kind. He didn't even know the players in a baseball game!"

I tried again.

"But, Eddie, don't you want, some day, to *be* something? You don't want to just—well—be always working at a job here or there. If you went to college—"

"Pa doesn't want me to go to college. He wants me to be another sniveling religious teacher, like Nat Breit. He'd like me to keep on working and go to his school at the same time, so that he can make me go with him afterwards to that desert dump Palestine that he thinks he'll be king of some time!"

"With *him*? What does he mean? How could he go? When could Papa go—unless he took us all with him?"

"Who knows what *he* means? I guess it's his 'dream.' Everybody over here thinks they have to have a 'dream.' "

"But now, look, Eddie,—don't you *hope* for something, what you'll be when you're grown up—?"

"Well,—Uncle Mark did talk to me. Uncle Mark—

113

he once wanted to be an artist. But he *likes* being a dentist. He thinks I could be a doctor, if I wanted to."

"You had good marks in school."

"He makes a good living. Aunt Sara said he could make much more, only he's always taking poor immigrant patients." Eddie laughed. "He says they have more interesting dental diseases."

I shuddered. "What's interesting about diseases?"

"Plenty, if you really think about it."

"I wish Uncle Mark had stayed an artist."

"Aunt Sara doesn't. She says she and the baby would have starved to death, so there'd have been a few more 'patchkes' hanging around on somebody's walls."

"I think they'd have been good."

"It's more use Uncle's a good dentist."

"Eddie, if you feel that way, maybe you could be a doctor. You don't want to stick at being a copyboy. Uncle Mark would plan it out for you. Go and see Uncle Mark again, Eddie. He'll tell you what to say to Pa."

Eddie looked thoughtful. "Well, I just might."

"Then maybe you should go after Pa today, go to his school, and put him in the right mood to you—"

"Like fun I will. I've got a date—going to go to the Culture Club. Those fellows are really living."

"Where—" But I didn't finish the question. I knew

this Club was mainly of high school boys, and they were sponsored by a gym teacher; they met only at each other's homes. Of course, there aren't any guarantees in life, but how much safer can you play? And I never heard that any of them got into trouble.

"What did you decide about going to high school now, Eddie? Pa says he'd rather you would go to school than work."

"I'm not going to depend on *him*. Every time he loses his temper he'll tell me to quit school and go to work. I'm better off sticking at the paper. I'll get a promotion. I'd like to be a reporter, maybe, some day."

"Don't you want to be educated, Eddie?"

"You mind *your* affairs, Sybil. I want to earn a salary and get the hell out of his house some day."

He slapped on his hat, then adjusted it in the mirror, gave himself a last critical glance, stooped and hastily retied one shoelace, then went smartly off. I wondered if he had new friends; I hoped they were not the wild sort.

I had been to Papa's school several times, sent by Mama with a message or to bring him a letter; I didn't usually go in to see him; I would hand whatever it was to the boy or girl in the outer lobby. But today I felt that I wanted to go in there, to see what his office was like.

I walked down broad Lenox Avenue, where the waving branches of the trees flurried and glittered and promised; I turned into 115th Street, narrow and crowded with children tumbling about the steps, crossed Fifth Avenue, where the expansive dignity of old private houses was made ridiculous by shabby store-fronts and scattered garbage and careless people, then down to the Roman magnificence of huge, dark arches of sooty brick, over which ran the trains, and, underneath, midst whiffs of old garbage and urine, the mad rush and scramble of the Sunday market-barrows. One had to keep watching alertly up and down the road when emerging on the other side of the market; an automobile might come by too fast to see a child.

Boys were running out of the doorway to the school; as I came near, I recognized Nat Breit dawdling beside an outer pillar, chatting with three or four other boys. He was tall, about seventeen years old, always with a hat on his smooth light hair; he had pale light eyes, a narrow, well-molded face with a narrow aquiline nose, and a dragging nasal voice.

He recognized me, I could tell, but made no sign; he finished his sentence, which involved the Torah, and listened to the answer or argument offered by another boy.

"Is my father in the office, Breit?" I asked, shyly.

116

"Who's your father?" popped another boy. "The janitor?" He didn't mean it rudely.

"Pipe down, dopey," said Breit, uncomfortably. "It's Mr. Raphel's daughter."

"Mr. Raphel—I thought you said she was kind of a blondie—dressed nice—don't she teach here a class?"

Breit had flushed slightly; now he went up the steps again, pushed open the double glass doors, and signaled me to come up. He held the door as I went inside.

He led me through a narrow corridor where boys and an occasional girl were moving about, and then with a soft knock immediately opened a door and held it. Papa was sitting at a much-littered desk, reading a notice or letter.

"Breit? Are the directors here already?" Then he saw me. He looked startled. "All right, Breit."

Breit went away.

"What's the matter?" Papa asked me, abruptly.

"Nothing. I—just thought I'd—come."

"But there's nothing for you here. You don't— you're not—" He was so obviously at a loss to account for me, that I felt ashamed at having come. Suddenly he stood up, went to a drawer of a large wooden file. He unlocked it with a key from his own key ring. He selected a set of papers and clipped them together.

"Look," he said. "You can help me. Here is a copy

of a plan—an idea I am putting forward for the Directors to approve. I believe it is a new idea in religious education. Your English is native. Can you read them and correct any errors in my English,—in half an hour?"

"Now?" I asked. I was always stimulated by a request for help.

"Now. Sit down—at that desk, in the corner."

I was elated. Conscious that my abilities entitled me to make a demand, I asked for a good pencil, with an eraser. I was thrilled with importance when Papa actually sharpened a pencil before handing it to me! I took the papers and the pencil, and sat down cheerfully to work.

At that moment there was a knock on the door; it opened, and a man stood there. Spick and span, white silk handkerchief, bright black boots, cheeks pink-shaven, dark hair slicked back. Papa's clothes were shabby, but still Papa had dignity, purpose. That fellow's a salesman, I thought, and almost laughed as Papa called him in. But now I saw he must be a teacher.

"Oh. Come in, Sattin." The name was so right, but it should have been the cheap kind, like sateen.

"New assistant, Mr. Raphel?" He grinned over at me.

118

"Have you been asked to attend the Directors' meeting?" Papa's voice was distinctly displeased.

"You know I haven't. You don't seem to like having me around when they come."

"Is there anything?" Papa's blue eyes were fixed meaningfully on Sattin's fulsome dark face.

Sattin handed Papa a couple of worn textbooks.

"I want you to give a look at these. My senior class, they need a new set of books. Take a look what they've got to contend with."

Papa handled the books, turned them over. He said, "As soon as the book covers get marked, you put in a requisition for new books! I've seen these; no pages torn out,—a rip here and there, some scribbling—." He handed them back to Sattin. "They're good for two more terms."

"You think appearances don't count. Smart boys don't like handling dirty, torn covers." Sattin shrugged. "That's why we don't get new pupils. —That a new pupil? They don't approve too many girls at the school. I thought your son was coming."

"Is that all, Sattin? I'm busy." Papa turned back to his papers. Sattin had been looking intently at me. Now he went out.

Papa read his mail, while I looked over his material. I came to his desk with it.

"How does it read?" he asked.

"Quite all right. Just a phrase here and there that isn't entirely idiomatic. Your Directors wouldn't even know."

Papa came home that night distinctly cheerful.

Mama asked him, "What did they say at the Directors' meeting? What do they think of your plan?"

"Approved," said Papa, with satisfaction. "Next week we begin."

Mama heaved a great sigh of relief. "Well, thank God," she said.

FOURTEEN

Little by little, the news of a novel teaching method, where children acted out the historic events and rites, began to go around the neighborhood. People began coming to the children's synagogue who had not been to an adult one for a long time. Papa was being congratulated. Not only that. Mr. Sattin, who had somewhere in his being the makings of a press agent, actually got some comments into the Jewish newspapers. And Papa was getting offers to head other schools.

All this added up to a raise. Our butcher, to his astonishment, was paid in full. This, being so unprecedented an act on the part of Mrs. Raphel, worried the man, and he came up to make sure he wasn't losing his customer. Our grocery order was almost doubled. He, on the contrary, came up to make sure that we were not planning a "skip," but Mama, to his astonishment, handed him a sizeable part of his

121

balance due. Lilie was presented with a very pretty blue dress with white embroidery. I was informed I might go and buy a dress. However, I didn't get it. I quite forget why not. Probably I didn't care; I had given up on clothes, and wanted only to read and to write. Or I bought concert tickets with the money.

More important: we now had a cleaning-woman come in twice a week to do the heavy work. Mama couldn't do much more than the cooking now; she had to hold on to furniture when she walked about the rooms; sometimes she fell and could not get up by herself.

Papa was going about, active and purposeful.

It seemed the Board of Directors had learned something from his participation idea. When Papa suggested that he might prepare dramatic representations by the children, of the basic festivals, beginning with Hanukkah, which was about three months off, they cautiously inquired whether the school could sell tickets and let in the "public." They were willing to assign half the profits to the school for a library Papa wanted, and half to Papa himself as payment for his extra work.

"Profits!" We nearly choked with laughter. But as long as the Board was willing to risk the expense of costumes, typing of parts, and extra lighting, labor, and so on, Papa agreed.

FIFTEEN

And Papa wrote a three-act play—short, of course. Lilie read it; he even showed it to me. The stories that had grown up around the holiday were indeed colorful and dramatic, full of grandly actable parts. Far from having difficulty finding girls and boys to perform, Papa had to assign the parts almost as rewards to the best students.

Thinking, no doubt, to interest Eddie at last in the Hebrew history, Papa offered him the role of the hero-general, Judah the Maccabee. Eddie's fine build and good looks would have graced the stage indeed. But Eddie had his job, and besides, his limp had become quite noticeable, and he didn't want to call attention to himself. He agreed to take charge of the ticket-selling at the box office to be set up in the school lobby; he was quick and accurate at figures.

The news got around, and early in December the

play, *Glory of Israel,* opened in the school basement, their only auditorium. There was actually an advance sale! The youngsters performed remarkably well. Hannah faced with martyr courage the death of her sons at the hands of the cruel Syrians; the Greek king thrust back his throne in a royal rage that really frightened some obstreperous kids running up the aisle; Judah raised his flag with a cry of defiance that thrilled the hall. All cheered!

By the third performance, it was clear that the play was a success, even at fifty cents a ticket, a high price for this clientele, many of whom saved the money by walking to and from their nearby work, or by adding an hour's piece work to the sweatshop jobs, or doing without the penny newspaper for a while. Not only the relatives of the performing children, but whole families, from tired old grandparents, their faces lighted up with pride and hope, to squealing little brothers and sisters, and babies who had been "napped" so they would stay awake.

Instead of running three nights, it ran seven, and could have run longer, except for the approach of yearly examinations at high school, which most of the pupils were attending.

On the last evening, a Saturday night, Lilie and I undertook to bring Mama. Her walking now was very slow and heavy, and for going out, to the doctor, or to visit—which she rarely did—Papa had obtained for her a second-hand wheelchair, which remained most of the time in the dark corner of the lobby of our tenement, almost out of sight.

Lilie dressed her, lending her her own new white silk blouse with French cuffs, and making a "halo" around her curly black hair and beautiful dark eyes, for once alight with pleasure, of her lovely ivory lace scarf, whose origin they both seemed to have forgotten. Papa was at the school; Lilie and I took turns wheeling her, and the traffic seemed to wait for us.

Eddie had insisted on going alone; he resolutely refused to be helped. We saw that he walked close to the buildings so that he could take hold of railings or rest against a wall. He went by himself to the school, but one night I followed him. I saw him getting himself up the entrance steps of the school—and that night it seemed to me I realized for the first time how many steps make four. As yet, we still dared not think too much about what might be wrong with Eddie.

I never saw Papa so energetic and happy as he was that Saturday night, when everyone applauded the final curtain, and the performers came crowding around him, still in their costumes, glowing at his praise. Mama and Lilie and I were near the stage, and Thad was up there making weird noises on the bugle that had been used to call up the Hebrew troops.

"Oh, aren't you *lucky* he's your Dad?" exclaimed the girl who had played Hannah, her oval face still brightly pink and her eyebrows blacked in around her large sentimental eyes. She held on to Papa's hand and to mine.

"I'm going to be a lawyer," said Judah the Maccabee, in his brazen helmet and red cloak. "But I'm always going to remember what Mr. Raphel told us, that we've got to take the honest side, not to disgrace our people."

Thad had come down among us. "I don't like Papa," he announced. "He spanks us."

"You ought to be ashamed to say that," said one of the mothers. "Your father's a great man!"

"I wish I had ten hours a week in Hebrew school instead of four," said the dark-faced "king," swinging his tinsel crown.

"Mr. Raphel wouldn't spank anybody!" said Hannah.

"Take Mama home," said Papa. He bent down and kissed her on the forehead; I couldn't recall ever seeing her so pretty and lively, her eyes shining, her cheeks pink with a natural flush, her beautifully shaped lips so relaxed with the happiness of the moment.

Eddie was still in the "box office" at the lobby, industriously sorting out, with the help of one of the

126

older pupils, the dollar bills, the rare fives, the halves, quarters, dimes, nickels, and even pennies. He used a drawer temporarily taken out of a desk in the office, and a large, black metal box which I had lent to Eddie because he needed a box with many compartments for the change. Papa watched him a while.

"Aren't you coming with us?" asked Papa, as Mama walked slowly and heavily into the lobby, to be settled in her wheelchair at the bottom of the four-step entrance. Lilie supported her on one side, Papa on the other, while the children who had come out with us glanced solemnly at each other.

"No, Papa," said Eddie. "I've got to finish checking, then I hand the money with the account to Klatzky here, and he and Weisser will take it away and carry it to the bank tomorrow."

"Looks like a profit," Papa smiled gleefully.

"The whole week's take sure will show profit. And tonight's been the biggest night," gloated Klatzky, a boy destined to become an accountant.

We were all asleep when Eddie's coming in, quite late, woke me for a little while. I wanted to ask him what the total receipts had been, but he had gone straight into the room he shared with Thad.

SIXTEEN

*

I had lent Eddie my black metal pencil box to keep the box-office change in. One morning, after Eddie had left, I happened to want some paper clips, and found them all mixed up together with rubber bands, hairpins, safety-pins, and the like, in a corner of my drawer of the bedroom dresser. I had taken them out of that box, and now I wanted it back, to put them in their own compartments again.

So I went into Eddie's room to get the box. I put my hand into the drawer and pulled it out. But something was blocking it. An awkward box of writing paper had become stuck in the opening, and I had to push it down with my fingers before the drawer opened enough to show the worn black enamel of the metal box.

At last it came out with a jerk that nearly dislodged it. And the box was full of money. Half-dollars, quarters, nickels, dimes, carefully arranged. I guessed the amount to be almost twenty dollars.

And then I remembered. I had heard Papa say something about having thought the total receipts from the play would be about twenty dollars higher than they turned out to be.

But surely Eddie had intended to bring the box to Papa, to whom the money partly belonged.

Only, then, why had he brought it home?

Why had he kept it in his drawer?

I pushed the drawer back, replacing it behind the writing paper.

I couldn't make up my mind what to do.

Ask Eddie? But if he hadn't mentioned it, nor given me back the box—it was nearly a week now—he didn't intend me to know.

At last, I thought of a way.

When Eddie came home, and had had something to eat, and he sat by the window in the front room, I came in and said, casually, not putting on the light,

"Oh, Eddie, you never gave me back my pencil box."

He started; it was too dark for me to see his face. This was as I wanted it.

"What do you need it for?" he grunted.

"Well, I want it, that's all. I want to put my pencils back in it."

129

"I'm using it," he said, curtly.

"Oh, Eddie!" I exclaimed, as if irritated.

"Well, get another one! I'll give you a quarter for it."

"You've got quarters?" I laughed. "But I like this one. It's large and has compartments." Then I dared. "What are you using it for?"

"Same as you."

"I'm going to go and get it, Eddie. It's mine."

He stood up quickly, stumbled, and exclaimed,

"If you go and get it, I'll never—"

But I went, and I got it. And he came stumbling and limping after me. I opened the drawer, took out the box, and then stood up, and placed it, closed, in his hands as he stood panting beside me. I had not put the bedroom light on, neither had he.

"Here it is, Eddie. It's real heavy. What have you got in it?"

"Oh!" He gave an exclamation of relief. He sat down on his bed, holding the box.

Then he spoke.

"Look, Syb. It may seem funny to you—but— Look. Pa made Lilie work for nothing, teaching one of the classes, for a year she got nothing."

"I know. I wouldn't have done it."

"Well—he wanted *me* to work for nothing, too. I told him, if I helped seven evenings at the school play,

130

that was like a job. A week's job. He said it wasn't. So
—I figured—I'd pay myself. Eighteen dollars is what
they'd have had to pay a cashier, an evening cashier.
So—I've got it—here."

"It—wasn't right, Eddie. But it wasn't really quite
wrong. Only you should have told Papa."

"*Tell* him! Are you crazy? He thinks everybody
should work for nothing at that old school of his.
Well, he can work for peanuts, and he can make Lilie,
but he can't make me. He never gives me anything.
If I work for someone and he doesn't pay me, it's just
the same, Pa or no Pa."

"Eddie, if you're right, if you're sure you're right,
you shouldn't be afraid to tell him!"

"What do you think,—he's going to say I'm right?"

"Suppose he finds out some other way? Suppose
that boy who helped, tells him something that—that
—well,—makes him ask you?"

Eddie sat there; I couldn't see his face, but he said
nothing for quite a while.

"All right," he muttered at last. "I'll tell him. I'm
not afraid of him."

Relief lifted my heart so much, I was almost happy.

"At least, if you tell him, he can't say you—you
took it!"

When I heard, the next evening, sounds of violent
argument from Eddie's room, and distinguished the

voices as Eddie's and Papa's, I came and stood outside to hear.

"—I had to render an accounting! Now I have to explain to them that twenty dollars was held back!" said Papa. He was angry, but not furious.

"All right! Can't you tell them I made a mistake? Half of it is yours, anyway!"

"Mistake!" Papa said grimly. "I do not like 'mistakes' in handling money, especially when the mistake appears to my advantage!" He added, pointedly, "I am not so sure that you *forgot*."

"All right! And what did *you* do that time in London, with my scholarship money? You know you bought a bicycle with it! And that money was given to us for *us*, not for our fathers!"

There was a moment's dead silence. Then Papa said,

"I can't believe what I hear you saying. What I did, with *your* scholarship money? How was that money yours? It was provided for the parents, to help in the support of the pupil."

"That's the way *you* saw it. All the other boys' fathers spent the money on the boys! You spent it for yourself!"

"You are wrong. Nevertheless, I will explain to you. At that time, I became—very—very troubled in my mind. The doctors advised me to find some way—

have a vacation. There was no hope for that. The doctors agreed that a bicycle might be the answer. I used the scholarship money for what appeared to be for the good of the family."

There was a silence. Then Eddie, sullenly,

"All right. It was still money I'd won. I didn't owe you anything. You didn't even give me the watch."

"You didn't owe me anything? Who housed, fed, clothed you since the day you were born?"

"Oh, I was waiting for that. I didn't ask to be born! You had to take care of me."

"Many fathers do not!"

"So you took money you thought you deserved. And I don't see any wrong in my taking this money that I earned."

"It is not the same thing!"

"You just don't see it my way!"

As the door flung open and Papa marched out, his lips angrily pressed together and the box closed tight, under his arm, I jumped out of sight. Eddie didn't get any of the money. Papa would have felt that Eddie had won the argument.

SEVENTEEN

There was something curious and puzzling about Eddie's limp. Sometimes it was so slight that he seemed to be going about much like other boys, except for what seemed to us to be some remaining effect of that bad fall he had in London, when he was carrying the pail of hot water. True, the doctor there had said Eddie fell because there was trouble with his legs, not the other way around. But we did not want to believe that.

Then, again, at other times the limping became so severe that it was noticeable to everybody; then he explained it as due to an accident, and it was taken for granted that he would get better soon.

It was probably with that expectation that he had been given the job at the newspaper. He liked the excitement, the rush, the boiling life of a great morning newspaper in New York City. Sometimes he thought, that if he got fully better, he would like to be a reporter.

The doctor to whom Mama was now being taken once a week by Lilie asked to see Eddie, too. And next time, Eddie went with them. The doctor talked to him a long time, and after examining him, asked him if he had ever thought of becoming a doctor himself. He suggested that Eddie might take up medical research, where he would not have to do much going about, but would work in a laboratory, associated with a hospital.

Eddie was instantly fired with this idea. He went along with Mama every time she saw Dr. Leame on a Saturday. And when I went with them, I could understand why. Dr. Leame was as gentle as Papa was hard with Eddie, and his interest and sympathy appeared real.

To do medical research, of course Eddie would have to finish high school and go to college. There was the rub. It would certainly be possible, if Papa would agree. Eddie's few dollars' contribution did not mean so much to the family now, since Papa's increase of salary. Also, I was working after school at the job Papa found me with the Hebrew Education Agency, where the easy-going boss was just as likely to tell me to take the afternoon off, if it was a nice day. Lilie was getting a small salary, too, teaching a Sunday class at Papa's school.

Dr. Leame was charging Mama a minimum fee, and for Eddie he did not charge at all. He said it was professional courtesy, since we had a doctor in the family, and one never knew when it would come in handy to have "pull" with a dentist! Eddie must have liked Dr. Leame because when he told us that terrible pun, Eddie laughed!

EIGHTEEN

I think it was about two months after the concert, that I came home from school one Friday afternoon to find Eddie sitting beside the window in the front room. It was much too early for him to have returned from work.

When he saw me, he waved, grinned, and began to chortle what seemed at first a humorous bit of doggerel:

> Hooray, hooray, Sam Binns is gonna be hung,
> Hooray, hooray, the measly son of a gun,
> He took away my jo-o-ob,
> Tee-doodle-oodle oo,
> When we're marching through Georgia.

His grin was not very deep, and the look in his eyes told me why he was turning it into a joke. Mr. Binns was management at the newspaper.

I came over and stood by him.

"What did you do, Eddie? Did you ask for a raise?" As if I didn't know, it was his physical condition. He seemed to catch at my suggestion.

"I was only getting twelve dollars a week—"

"Oh! Pa thought—Pa said it was eight—"

"As if I'd tell him. He always makes me give him what he thinks is the whole thing, then he just gives me back carfare and coffee money. I never told him it was twelve."

"He makes Lilie give him her pay envelope. I thought you gave him yours, too."

"Like fun . . . I told him they don't put it in an envelope.—Anyway—I—I asked for fifteen."

I knew it wasn't true. But I knew he couldn't bear the shame of telling me he was fired. And it wasn't just shame; it meant he would be admitting something he couldn't face: that he wasn't physically able to hold that job any more.

"So Mr. Binns said, they liked me and all that stuff, but he couldn't just raise me and not the others. So" —and this I felt was *it*—"he said I wasn't getting around fast enough, and I asked him if there wasn't a clerking job where I could sit at a desk, and he said there was only a mail room job, and I'd have to stand all day for that—so—"

I couldn't think what to say next. I simply stood

still. Lilie was going to get a raise soon. I was still working part-time in the Education Agency office, twelve hours a week at forty cents an hour alphabetizing cards. But the boss was beginning to put his hand on mine, and telling me pretty girls shouldn't have to work. I answered that I wasn't pretty, but somehow that seemed to cheer him up no end. Anyway, I had a feeling my job wasn't going to last long.

"Don't tell Pa yet," he warned me. "I saved the difference—some of it. I'll give him the eight dollars for about another two weeks. By that time I'll have a job. One of the boys there knows a printer who needs someone to spell. I didn't go to school much, I know, but I *can* spell."

Here was something I could smile about, because he *could* spell.

"O. K.," I said, sitting down, "spell 'meticulous.'"

"How do *you* know that word?" he chaffed.

"Come on. Spell it."

"I, t."

"Oh—come on!"

"Me, tickle, us."

I guessed he thought I doubted his ability. I didn't want him to think anything like that, especially since I knew he was good at spelling.

"Well, when are you going to see that printer? Couldn't you make it this week?"

"Sure. I'm going to."

He got the job. But he had to walk up four flights and down four flights twice a day. And he couldn't do it.

Lilie had talked to Papa about Eddie's illness, but Papa didn't seem to be saying anything, or planning to do anything. He was supposed to go and consult with the doctor whom Uncle Mark had recommended—a bigger man than Dr. Leame. This was Dr. Elpert, a well-known neurologist. But Papa hadn't gone.

At last I stopped Papa just as he was going out; he had come home unexpectedly that evening for supper, and Mama had managed to prepare a cheese omelet; there was a pear and some rye bread, and lemon tea.

"Papa," I said, almost at the door—he was trying to avoid me—"Papa, Uncle Mark wants you to go to see Dr. Elpert."

"I am fully occupied at the school! I have no time for useless visits!"

"But Papa—this is *important!* It's—about *Eddie!* You don't know what Dr. Elpert might say. Maybe—"

"I am not a doctor! He does not need to consult with me!"

"But—it's Eddie's *health*—"

Papa stood still.

"The health of the children is in the domain of the wife and mother," he declared. "I am the bread-winner."

And he went out and shut the door behind him, adding as he went,

"I do not believe his matter is serious. The doctors are building it up for their own reputations!"

NINETEEN

Without a job, Eddie sat around the house getting gloomier and gloomier. He had had to tell Papa, of course. Papa was sure it was because of something Eddie had done. The only thing that now interested Eddie was getting to the library, where he would sit for hours reading medical books. I told this to Papa, to put him in the mood for Dr. Leame's suggestion that Eddie become a medical researcher.

Papa shrugged impatiently.

"A whim. He'll get tired of it. He doesn't understand what he's reading."

"Well, no, I guess not. But he's not prepared to yet."

"He never will be."

But Lilie and I made up our minds that Eddie must have a straight discussion with Papa about it. We made Papa agree to an appointment with Eddie, for a "serious talk," at a time when there could be no interruptions and no previous meeting or business at the school.

The time chosen by Papa was Sunday noon, after his breakfast; he did not have to be at school till three. Lilie wouldn't be home yet from her Sunday class, but I planned to be about, just in case.

I made Eddie dress neatly; he had been getting careless. Now he looked well in his brown suit, with brown boots. I had bought him a new dark green tie, and he tied it carefully . . . Alas, when I saw it the last time . . . ! I tied his bootlaces, though he didn't like to let me, but I wanted the knots to hold, and Eddie was fumbling too much with his hands nowadays.

I followed Eddie, though quietly and at a distance, into the front room, where Papa was sitting in the Morris armchair of smooth black wooden slats and maroon corduroy long-cushioned back. He was reading his "Sunday Times."

"Papa."

"Yes?" A pause. Eddie began in high style, like the way Papa talked when he was impressing people with his ideas on religious education.

"Papa. I have a feeling—everybody ought to do something useful in the world. Something they have to work hard at,—prepare themselves for."

143

Papa was skimming the newspaper with his eyes.
"Well?" He did not even look at Eddie.

"Well, you know, Papa, just as you decided to become a teacher of religion, and all that—" Eddie hesitated. "Well—"

Papa sneered from within the newspaper. "You don't mean that *you* want to teach—"

"Oh, no. I couldn't. I'd—never—be as good as you. But—Mama being sick—and my own case—Dr. Leame talked to me—and I've been to see Uncle Mark about it, and he feels the same—and they'll help—"

Papa turned the broad leaf of the newspaper and skimmed the headlines.

"Pa!"

"Go on. I'm listening to you."

"But—you're reading—"

"I hear you perfectly." He turned another page.

"I know now what I want to be."

"You know? Good. You will soon have to go seriously to work, to earn a living, not merely to depend upon me."

"Papa, I want to be a medical researcher."

Now Papa put down the paper. He got to his feet, put his hands in his pockets, walked towards the window, turned his heavy, square head to the glass panes.

144

"A medical researcher. Yes. This is an excellent ambition."

I nearly squawked with surprise, over in my corner. Papa was going to encourage him! I had expected an onslaught.

"A medical researcher," said Papa, "helps humanity. He is a necessary part of our civilization. He is a vital aid in the essential profession of medicine. A medical researcher can earn an independent living. There are requirements, of course."

Eddie stepped forward, an eager, grateful warmth enlarging his eyes.

"I know. I'd have to study a lot. I have to finish high school first. I could work while I study. Dr. Leame has all the books; he'll lend them—the heavy ones I can read in his own library. He said maybe there'd be work he would need—he'd pay me—"

Papa turned, faced Eddie fully, spoke right into his eyes.

"*You* cannot be a medical researcher."

Eddie gasped.

"I—"

"*You* have not the brains."

"I—but how can you—"

"How can I tell? I see hundreds of boys. Do you think I do not yet know how to tell what stuff a boy is made of? *You* cannot concentrate. *You* cannot ob-

OUR EDDIE

serve. *You* cannot make necessary distinctions. You will not succeed."

Eddie's whole face seemed to crumple; his eyes went out and were dull.

"He *has* brains!" I blurted out, furiously. "There's nothing the matter with Eddie's brains! He won a scholarship, didn't he, when none of his friends did! He—"

"And could not even remain a messenger boy. He loses every job. His excuse is always that he limps. But what are the *true* reasons?"

"Dr. Leame thinks he can! Uncle Mark thinks he can!"

"A medical researcher!" Papa flamed out in rage. "For this he needs college! Who will support him? Dr. Leame? Uncle Mark? He is already seventeen!"

"High school! And he said he'd work part time! It's only two years! And they said they'd help—"

Suddenly Papa turned upon Eddie.

"Become a teacher!" he shouted. "Become a teacher! In this I can help you! In this you can succeed! You will have my example before your every day—"

Eddie burst out. "A teacher! Why don't you *say*, a *Hebrew* teacher? I should work for nothing, like Lilie did a whole year?"

Through the yelling, came from the other room the

146

bewitching, melting tones of a great tenor, suddenly in the middle of the final aria of *Lohengrin,* on our installment-bought phonograph. Even Eddie and Papa had to halt their mingling fury. But only for a few bars.

Now Papa began again, on an entirely different note. Quietly, almost persuasively, almost appealingly, he said,

"Why can't you see so simple a fact? Hebrew teaching is not going to remain as it is now. We are in America, now, a land of freedom, where the Jewish communities, like those of other groups, are constantly strengthening, rising, with the affluent society of which they are also a part."

Eddie was tightening his lips and looking from under his eyelids at Papa's face, now almost calm in exposition.

"Where there is now one poor little Talmud Torah, by the time you are ready to teach there will be ten. They will no longer be growing out of little groups of immigrant children, gathered around a steampipe in a tenement basement with their Rabbi, one tattered book among them; they will be real schools. Not on a few rented floors of a deserted old office building, like my school today; they will be specially built, light classrooms, wide corridors, a library, proper plumbing, sufficient heat. And teachers will no longer be ill-paid.

An affluent business community cannot afford to show the world poverty-stricken religious schools. It will tax itself to provide good salaries—"

Eddie's face was hard with resentment and suspicion.

"That's what *you* think. For *Hebrew*—that's deader than Greek you wouldn't let Lilie take!"

Papa's face grew red and convulsed, and I awaited thunder. But he controlled himself as I had never seen him do before.

"It is not only the language. There is the great literature, the wisdom and culture of thousands of years of noble minds—"

"Very noble," Eddie sneered. "The grocer here wouldn't trust me for a sandwich when he heard my father was a Hebrew teacher—and *he's* a Jew—"

Papa nearly broke, but not quite. "Have you ever heard of the Balfour Declaration? England favors a Jewish homeland in Palestine. America favors it! Thousands of Jews are returning to rebuild the land of Israel into a land of refuge for the scattered people. They will till the soil, they will build cities, Hebrew will be spoken again in the streets and in the homes, it will be a living language!"

"I've heard your speeches before—"

"You do not know—I am purchasing a strip of land—"

"In *Palestine?*"

"I am purchasing in *your* name—a dollar a week for five years—"

"A strip of dirty sand and pebbles five thousand miles away! Why didn't you buy it in Texas? They've got oil there—"

Papa slapped Eddie in the face.

Eddie grew white as paper. For a few moments he could not move his leg, though he was trying to walk. Then he swung his hip till it propelled his bad leg forward, and, pushing my help aside, he limped out.

Papa saw me then. I couldn't help crying.

All this time, the deep, melodious singing had gone on. Papa went into the other room and snapped the record needle off in the middle of a word. I caught a glimpse of Lilie's resentful eyes as she turned her head away. She must have been standing there the whole time.

This time every word Papa had said about the future of the Jews came true. That "strip of dirty sand" became part of the site of one of the most modern cities in the world, and Hebrew began to be spoken as a living language.

But by that time, Papa was ashes in the hillside of the Mount of Olives, in the Old City of Jerusalem.

TWENTY

"Come on," said Lilie.

It was late in the afternoon; I had come home and made tea—we still had that habit—for me and Eddie. Mama was asleep, Papa of course at his school.

"Where to?" I asked.

"Aren't you going to your class at the school?" Eddie wanted to know.

"Don't have anything to eat," Lilie warned.

Ed put down his sandwich, but I finished my raisin cake.

"You're so greedy!" said Lilie irritably. "Now you'll turn up your nose at Aunt Sara's. We're invited to early supper there tonight, and you'd better be polite and eat what you get. I don't know how you live, you never want to eat real food."

"Aunt Sara?" repeated Eddie. "You mean she's remembered we're alive?"

"Look, she invites us every once in a while,—one of us. It's not too bad."

"Must be the maid's night off," grinned Eddie.

"She wants to talk to us. She said it's something special."

"I'll have to come late. Got to drop off a book I borrowed from Dr. Leame."

"Don't be too late."

"All right," Eddie said.

Aunt Sara met us in the hall of her apartment. Her hair had just been coiffed, she wore a formal black silk dress, with a small gold pin on the shoulder. I assumed we were intended to disappear before an evening reception of more important people.

"Where's Eddie?" She lightly kissed Lilie and me.

"He's returning a book to Dr. Leame. It's quite near; he won't be long."

Aunt Sara clicked her tongue.

"This Raphel family," she said in a tone of expected endurance. I noticed that the huge rubber plant in the hall had been washed down. "Come into the dining room.—Lou! The girls are washing their hands."

"Yes, ma'am."

The handsome bathroom was in shining order.

"Don't use the hand towels," warned Lilie. A small army of them, with embroidered corners smartly

151

showing, were ranged, each half-over the next, on a towel rack.

"I know!"

We sat down at a small table, set for four simple meals, to one side of the dining room. Lou, her strangely beautiful black face looking like an African wood sculpture, smiled warmly at us as she came in bearing a platterful of hot pancakes and a boat of mushroom sauce; we were hastily digging into the half-grapefruits on our plates.

"Oh—ain't yuh brother comin'?" she asked.

"He is a Raphel. He will be late," said Aunt Sara.

"I'll take back his pancakes an' keep 'em hot—"

"Never mind. They taste good cold, too. Don't mix things up in the kitchen for the guests . . . Uncle Mark would have been here. Lilie, we have something special to talk with you about. But he forgot when he told me to invite you tonight, he forgot that this is the night when Claire is playing violin at a party, and he will have to bring her home. Some of their guests are coming here afterwards."

It didn't feel pleasant, to know something "special" was to be discussed, yet to be squeezed in between Eddie's lateness and an early dismissal.

"So we'll begin now," said Aunt Sara, as Lou handed around the pancake platter. "Your family are the most *impossible* people I have ever known! What

are you *doing* about your brother?" She didn't let
Lilie answer. "What is Ezekiel waiting for? About
your mother—! that is already a lost cause. But after
all, *her* life is"—she shrugged her ample shoulders—
"take away the grapefruit, Lou—*her* life is completed.
But Eddie is a young man—a boy! Ezekiel will wait
till men come in white jackets to carry his eldest son
into a home for chronic invalids!"

"Do you think we haven't been doing everything
we can? You know Dr. Leame's been trying—" exclaimed Lilie.

"Dr. Leame! He is a beginner! For such a condition
—didn't Uncle give you a letter for Dr. Elpert? *There*
is a doctor. A neurosurgeon. A great specialist in
spinal pathology."

"Papa won't go," I said.

Aunt Sara looked incredulous. "Dr. Elpert is willing
to examine Eddie—Uncle telephoned him about it—
he charges fifty dollars an examination—for your
uncle's nephew it will be courtesy—and Papa won't
go? This I could not have thought possible." She was
almost pale. "Lou, take away the dishes. When Eddie
arrives, you'll bring in coffee and cake." She waited till
Lou had left, then went on.

"If this is multiple sclerosis—it is not sure yet—
there will be creeping paralysis! Unless an operation
by Dr. Elpert can save him—do you know what is be-

fore this boy? First the legs, then the arms,—you will have to send him then to the hospital—"

"He's got a home, Aunt Sara!" I cried out. "And as long as Lilie and I are in it, Eddie'll be in it, too!"

"A home! How long can he still live in a home? Do you understand that he will become heavy, a dead weight? Who will manage his natural functions? You will not be able to lift him, not even turn him around —he will first be in a chair, then in a bed, helpless. Then, his speech will be affected—his eyesight—"

"Stop it, Aunt Sara!" Lilie said, with self-control. "We don't know yet—"

"And how do you propose to find out, if your father cannot find time to go to Dr. Elpert?" Aunt Sara was silent for a moment with sheer frustration.

"Such parents," she said at last.

But I gave a cry of shock, and jumped to my feet.

There at the entrance to the dining room stood Eddie.

Eddie, pallid, almost green in the light just over his head, Eddie with his shoulders trembling, Eddie with his mouth trying in vain to open. One hand was jerking.

Aunt Sara had turned around at my cry, and now *she* saw Eddie. She grew suddenly pale. Lilie and I went up to Eddie and made him sit down. He was breathing hard. Aunt Sara called, her voice shaking a little.

"Lou! Bring him coffee!" Then she said to Eddie, "We weren't talking about—you, Eddie. We were talking about what *might* be—in certain cases. Not in your case. The doctors haven't even decided what your case is." She managed to smile. "You Raphels are always imagining things!"

Eddie's color began to come back.

"I—didn't hear—the first part. Just the—rest of it." He took up the cup of hot coffee Lou had almost instantly set down by his plate, her face wrinkled with sympathy, but put it down again before drinking any, to say,

"Yes.—Yes, you see, I know it isn't my case. I've had all the examinations. They don't know what it is. But it isn't—that. See—I've got the proper knee reflex." He shoved his chair aside to give himself space. He struck his left knee sharply with the stiffened flat of his hand; the foot kicked out in the normal way. "See? It's O. K." He repeated the gesture with his right knee, but the right foot remained motionless. He disregarded it. "Look, the other test. I can touch my nose with my hand." He swiftly touched his nose, once, twice, three times. The fourth time his hand went wildly staggering, never reaching higher than his chest.

155

"See? Three times out of four!"

A deadly sickness settled on my heart, that I felt would never leave me any more.

"It could be any kind of nervous attack," Eddie went on. "It doesn't have to be—anything special."

Aunt Sara spoke after a minute or two.

"Lilie," she said, quietly, "tomorrow morning you'll call up this number." She gave her a card. "You'll make an appointment for as soon as he'll give you one. Don't wait with it; Dr. Elpert is going to Europe in a few weeks, he'll be six months there."

Lilie spoke then. "I'll call Dr. Elpert tomorrow. But I spoke to him already. Uncle Mark told me to."

"Oh? What did he say?"

"From—what he's heard,—what Dr. Leame said,— he—well, he agrees with Eddie. He doesn't think it's anything specific."

Eddie's face brightened incredulously.

"He doesn't think it'll need any—extreme measures. He says—nobody can say for sure what it is."

Aunt Sara stood up, and we all got up to go. She smoothed back her flat light brown hair over her forehead, then wiped her face with her open hand. As she said goodnight to Eddie, she hesitatingly straightened his dark green tie a little, though it didn't need straightening. I looked back and saw her heave a deep sigh.

She didn't believe what Lilie had said.

But Eddie did, and that was the important thing.

Papa still refused to take any part in Eddie's contacts with doctors. "Your aunt's meddling doesn't alter my opinion," was all he said. In a way, it relieved Eddie. It seemed to strengthen his hope.

Lilie telephoned Dr. Elpert. He made an appointment. Eddie went to his office with Lilie. I was afraid to go. Now we had to await his diagnosis, which he told us would be mailed to Papa after he had studied the findings.

The letter came. Papa gave it, unopened, to Lilie, and walked away. Mama was not told about the new step we had taken; she was hardly able to walk at all, there was no use in telling her, at least until we knew something definite.

TWENTY-ONE

Lilie and I walked to school together, one morning a week later.

"You'll have to come with me after school today," she said.

"I promised a girl in my class I'd help her with her Latin. She's going to flunk the term."

"Let her flunk."

"What's it about?"

"Dr. Elpert. Pa got a letter from him. He won't operate on Eddie. He says he doesn't know for sure what the disease really is."

It stopped me still, in the middle of crossing Seventh Avenue. A boy on a bicycle swerved sharply to avoid hitting us, and a bus had to brake hard to avoid hitting the boy.

"Stupid thing!" Lilie snapped at me.

"Get up on that curb, will you, miss!" yelled the bus driver.

Lilie pulled me across to the curb.

"We've got to see Dr. Elpert. We've got to talk him into performing the operation," Lilie declared.

"But how can *you* tell if an operation will help?"

"There's nothing else to do. I can't push two wheel-chairs," Lilie said with finality.

"As if you'd have to! But *he* must know why he won't!"

"He wants to get out of it. We haven't got money. He was paid fifteen hundred dollars the other time."

"Fif-teen hun-dred—"

"He saved *that* man. They had money. No one's going to bother with *us* if they can help it."

"How do you think you're going to make him?"

"You'll see."

I didn't go with her. She decided I'd be more hin-drance than help, and she'd go it alone.

And she did.

Three days later, Lilie told me,

"Dr. Elpert'll operate."

"He will? You *made* him promise?"

"Yes, I did."

"But how could you make him?"

"I told him I knew it was because we couldn't pay.

159

And I told him I'd tell everybody, everywhere, that he wouldn't help because we didn't have the money."

"What did he say?"

"He said he had no reason to conclude that Eddie's condition was similar to the other man's. He was not convinced that drainage of spinal fluid for relief of pressure would have any good effect."

"But the symptoms—aren't they the same?"

"That's what I told him. He said they were superficially the same, but they were only symptoms, they didn't prove the cause was the same. He said there was a fifty-fifty chance. He said I didn't have the right to decide—"

"Fifty-fifty what?"

"That Eddie'd live. He said, if it didn't cure, it would probably kill."

"Are you going to tell Eddie *that?*"

"The doctor is. He said he was going to put it to him straight. And if he chose the operation, Papa'd have to sign it, and he'd operate, free.—He asked me where the hell Pa was. He said he'd never heard of such a thing,—a father letting his daughter take over in a thing like that. I said Papa couldn't get away from his school. I thought Dr. Elpert would have a heart attack himself, when he heard that. He said the whole thing was—"

She shrugged her shoulders and turned up her large green eyes.

"So it is," I said. "But—I *don't* think it means Pa doesn't care. I think it means, he doesn't *want* to believe it. He can't *bear* to believe it."

"The doctor asked me, 'Is that his *son?* Not his stepson? Adopted? His real *son?*' He couldn't believe me."

"Pa never went to the hospital to fetch Thad, after the kid had his tonsils out. When the letter came to get the kid, he left it on a dresser. When I found it I grabbed my wool scarf and went to the hospital, but Thad had simply walked out all by himself and gone home. Without even a scarf to wind around his throat," I remembered. "Pa can't face these things."

"Let's get upstairs." Lilie looked very tired.

We came up and into the front room.

"Who sent the daffodils?" I asked. "Do you know?"

"Oh, I brought them." Lilie went over to the circular blue earthenware bowl. She rearranged the flowers a trifle. "Isn't this blue pure heaven? And I found it in Woolworth's. The only one this shade. And it simply cries for daffodils, and just this one narcissus."

Kill or cure. The wearying cruelty of it! Who had organized life that way? God? Or was it our own

161

stupidity? But why we were made unknowing? The fear! the grief!

"Oh, Lilie!" I cried at last. "Can't we just let him alone?"

Mama had become so weak and pale in the meantime that the doctor was called in to see her. He advised a change of air and complete rest, for at least a month. Papa did not like the idea; he knew he would find life difficult without her. But he gave in. One of his pupils had relatives who owned a homey boarding-house in the country, just a few miles out of the city. Papa wrote to them, and they agreed to take her for a very small charge, although they knew she was a semi-invalid.

It was sad without Mama around. Eddie missed her even more than we did, perhaps. But I think Lilie and the doctor had planned it for this time, so that Mama would not have to see Eddie go away.

TWENTY-TWO

And the day came when Eddie was taken to the hospital. He was to rest three days, before the operation. Lilie went along, taking charge of his wheelchair. I walked beside, helping to get him into the chair and out of it again.

I went the next day to visit.

While the male nurse took care of Eddie's needs, I went outside, and another patient, a man some years older than Eddie, wheeled himself out into the hall to chat with me.

"Your brother's got real guts," he said. "The doctor didn't use kid gloves when he talked to him. He laid it on the line. And Eddie took it that way. Maybe I shouldn't have told you that . . ."

"It's all right," I said. "I know."

"Eddie said, 'Doctor, if I have to stay this way, getting worse all the time, I'd rather go.' I wish I had his guts."

The man's eyes were straining at me, good gray eyes, suffering like a dumb animal's. I could feel what he would have wanted to say. He wanted me to think him brave, but he wanted me, too, to know the injustice, the cruelty, of illness. I knew. Of course I knew. But what do you *say?* What on earth do you say? I just looked at him. We knew each other's thoughts. I was afraid of his eyes. I knew he was mutely begging me to feel something about him, even for that moment, even while we were strangers, to feel as though he were a total person, an ordinary man.

I forced myself to smile at him. But it couldn't work. He gazed at me for a hard minute, then turned his face aside, and let his eyes close. I never even knew his name.

I went to school the day of the operation. I felt as if I'd go out of my mind if I didn't.

I couldn't wait for the hospital to call our house. As soon as I knew the operation was over, I telephoned. They didn't know the answer yet. I telephoned again, still from school.

At last they said there was a report. I stood, trembling, in the pay-station phone booth, the phone shaking in my hand.

A man's voice . . . a cold, sad, voice, like a winter's day . . . like the end of a winter's day . . . Eddie had died.

I didn't go home. I didn't go to the hospital.

I found myself walking up Riverside Drive, along the open side, rough with stones and rocks, that led up to Grant's Tomb. I watched a freight train below the cliff as it rumbled by on its way down to the warehouses at Twelfth Avenue.

To my right as I walked numbly in the spring sunlight ran the line of great apartment buildings that rimmed the western edge of the city.

Something drew my eyes abruptly upward as I reached One Hundred and Sixteenth Street, towards the roof of a palace-like apartment house. By some trick of reflection, the late sun snatched at a French window being closed, high up near the sky. For one moment only it whirled into a triple dance of blazing ovals, violently rayed above and below with golden light.

It was so strange, so brief and so unbelievably beautiful,—as though Eddie had waved to me, from

165

wherever he was now. Or as though Creation had stopped to flash me a signal of hope. I only say, that is how it seemed to me.

III
HAL

TWENTY-THREE

New York! I had never seen it before!

Here we were, sailing in on a great ocean liner, into this magnificent bay. It was still spring; it was getting into twilight, when suddenly all that mass of looming buildings that had been moving slowly towards us— as it seemed—burst into thousands of lights, glittering all over!

Mom went "O-o-oH!"

Dad laughed.

"Boy!" he said, leaning on the rail. "New Yorkers don't know what they've got! If they had to travel three thousand miles for a sight like this, they'd go. But they've got it around the corner, so they don't think anything of it!"

We had dinner at the Waldorf Astoria, on West 34th street, "swellest place in town." Dad had done all right in England. We went through Pennsylvania Station on our way; I wanted to see those magnificent arcades of solid pillars, the mighty swing of the entrance, and that superb sweep of interior dome. The Europeans may sniff at American architecture, but I don't see where their Colosseum or triumphal arches can beat what we have here, except in the surroundings and the beautiful approaches. I plan to study architecture—going to be an architect, I hope—so I notice these things more.

Dad found us a suitable apartment, which was no small feat on his part; they were pretty scarce at that time. Mom thought seventy-five a month a bit steep, but Dad was doing well; he liked the open spaces around Grant's Tomb. Mom said it would be the Arctic regions in winter, when those winds got blowing across the Hudson River. But when Dad had his mind made up, he almost always got his way,—chiefly, I figured, because he was usually ninety percent right. Besides, I was going to enter Columbia University that fall, provided I passed the entrance exams; I'd be practically on campus. So Mom said O.K. It was at 119th Street and Riverside Drive.

I was planning on becoming an architect, even then. I spent my free time taking long walks around the city; sometimes I went with the Columbia postgrad who was helping me brush up for the exams, but he hated New York. Couldn't see any beauty in it. So I had to go by myself. It got to be lonely.

One thing disappointed me no end.

I had been looking forward to meeting the Raphels again when we got to New York. I had written to Eddie a couple of times while I was going to school in Edinburgh; he had sent me a card, then a short letter, not saying much; then we sort of forgot about writing. When I got here, I didn't have any of the cards—there had been a Christmas card from Sybil, but she had not given any address.

Of course I had depended on the telephone book, but when I looked them up, I couldn't find their name. I thought they must have moved away.

I remembered they had lived near Mr. Raphel's school in London; they would probably have arranged it the same way in New York. Dad suggested, "Look up the Hebrew religious schools in the phone book, and call them. You might hit on the right one; anyway one of their principals might know Mr. Raphel."

There were quite a few in the lower East Side, which was mostly Jewish. But none of them knew. Then Mom said, "Wasn't he in some kind of movement—you told us, some back-to-Palestine idea he was always talking about—"

So I started hunting under Zionist. And that was it.

171

A women's branch of the organization had Lilie's name and address; a friend of hers was called to the phone and told me they were on the fourth floor, it was near 115th Street, one block west of Fifth Avenue, but it was called Lenox Avenue, not Sixth Avenue. She didn't think they had a telephone.

I didn't want to wait till I got an answer by mail; knowing they were always informal, I just went there.

The neighborhood had been a lot better than it was now, that was easy to tell, because the avenue was very broad and planted with trees along both sides of the street; but most of the apartment-house fronts had been made into small stores. The people were mostly shabby-looking. One side street,—110th Street, it was,—was full of wheelbarrow peddlers lined up at both curbs, selling foods, cold drinks, trifles of all kinds. The noise, the kids, the women, the rubbish underfoot, added up to mixed languages, lots of immigrants, neglected houses, low rents.

So I figured the Raphels hadn't come very far up. I decided to bring Mrs. Raphel some flowers. I looked for a florist's, but I had to go to 116th Street, which was a wide cross street with better stores. I couldn't find anything there but gaudy set-pieces, wedding and birthday stuff.

So I settled for a corsage of pink rosebuds.

The houses on this block were four-floor tenements, not too old; they had broad windows and electric lighting; the entrances were narrow, the lobbies small. I started up the steps two at a time; at the top of the first flight there were two doors. One had no name, the other had a Jewish name that was not Raphel.

I rapped on the door that had no name, and pressed the bell. There was no answer, so I tried the handle. The door was unlocked. I opened it slightly, and glanced in. The narrow hallway showed a large room to the side, its door open; and that room had the casual, half-charming, half-untidy look characteristic of the Raphel home in London.

Still no one came. I wondered if they could all be out. That didn't seem likely, at five o'clock, with the outer door unlocked.

I walked rather quickly down the hall, past other open rooms, all having that look of half-achieved, half-frustrated attractiveness.

Suddenly, at the entrance to the dining room, I came face-to-face with an elderly man.

I couldn't be sure at first who it was.

He seemed suddenly stricken pale, quaking, his hand trembling on a chair-back which he seemed to have grasped for steadiness.

"Oh," he said. "Oh." Embarrassed, he was trying

to smile. It was Mr. Raphel. Shabbier, shorter, with gray in his black hair and short, pointed beard and mustache. But that was not the real change. His deep-set blue-gray eyes now looked sunken, sad and unsure.

"I thought—I thought—You are—" he seemed to search for my name.

"I'm Hal Kent, sir," I said, putting out my right hand. He shook my hand, and seemed to hold on to it for support. "Er—I'm awfully sorry," I apologized. "I shouldn't have marched in like that. But the bell didn't ring, and the door was open. You must have thought I was a burglar!"

He dropped my hand. "No. It wasn't that. But—it sounded like—I mean, a young man's footsteps—suddenly, like that. I was thinking of—Eddie. That was how he used to come in—before. I—for a minute, I almost thought it was he." He coughed.

"Take a seat," he said, and sat down himself. "You are very tall now. I remember you. London. Three years now." I sat down by the table.

"I suppose Eddie will be home soon," I ventured.

"Eddie!—" He gasped. "I—I thought they wrote you . . . Eddie . . . he's . . . dead."

He didn't say any more.

I was so shocked, I could not get myself together to say anything, not even a word of conventional regret.

"Sybil will be home soon. Lilie has a job; it keeps her rather late."

"When did he—" I didn't finish the sentence; it sounded unreal. I saw Dusty Heap in front of me, Eddie smacking the ball with his cricket bat, tossing the bat down and making his count of runs while the catcher ran after the still-flying ball . . . Eddie's alert eyes, his sturdy body . . . his roughish, good-natured voice . . . Dead?

"Some weeks now . . . Sybil will talk to you."

I stood up. "I'll go down and wait for her in the street, then." I felt Mr. Raphel would rather I did that.

"As you please," he said. "Thank you for coming." He shook hands again, this time very briefly, and I went. I was still holding the corsage of rosebuds, wrapped in green paper.

I walked slowly downstairs. Turning into the lobby at the foot of the steps—it was dark there though still bright outside, I brushed against a girl who was coming up.

She gave a cry.

"I'm so sorry," I began. "Did I hurt—"

"*Hal!*"

It was a young girl, thin but full-bosomed, with large dark eyes, boyish-cut hair, and a sudden smile that somehow made her beautiful for a moment.

175

"Syb . . . Of course. It's Sybil!"

She seized my arms with her hands and exclaimed, "I wouldn't have known you! . . . So *tall!* . . . I am so glad! . . . Come on up! Have you been upstairs?"

"Yes . . . your father's there . . ."

"Oh. But—oh, Hal—"

"I know about Ed . . . He told me . . ."

"Yes." She winced. "But Hal, you know, Pa's not— I mean, he's—well, it's as though some hard casing on him has cracked. He's different . . ."

"Let's go out. Let me take you to tea, in the neighborhood somewhere . . . or dinner . . ."

"I'll have to go up first, tell him I'm back."

"Will he worry? He never used to, did he?"

"Well—I think he might. I'd better tell him."

In a few minutes she came down, carrying a scarf. As we went into the street she said,

"He was sitting with his head in his hands. He keeps on worrying now, about what he *should* have done . . . now, when it doesn't matter any more!" she ended sharply. Then she drew a heavy sigh.

"Is there a restaurant nearby—one you like?" I asked her. She was quite pale and thin, but she threw the red scarf around her head; it rimmed her face with life.

"Oh," she said. "On 116th Street. I haven't been in

176

it yet, but it looks nice. I think it's too early for dinner."

"Let's try it."

So we went to the tearoom. All the way we didn't say a word. We went inside and sat down at one of the tables. It was pleasant in there. The walls were painted with pastel murals in green and flower colors, suggesting a spring garden.

I asked the waitress for English tea, with toasted muffins and strawberry jam, to remind Sybil of old times. That was stupid of me; it made us feel more sharply that Eddie was gone.

"Can you talk about it yet?" I asked.

"I'd rather," she answered simply. "You were his friend."

The waitress was setting the tea; everything was on the table.

"Have tea first," I suggested. "With muffins and jam."

"All right."

"We'll have some of those beautiful, beautiful pastries." I smiled, she did too.

"Afterwards," she said.

She poured the tea. I poured the hot water. The lid was loose; some of the boiling water leaped out, the bubbles bursting on my hand. Syb gave a cry and hastily wiped them off with her napkin.

"But that's nothing, Syb!" I was surprised. There were sudden tears in her eyes. "It only hurt for a second!"

"Oh—oh, I know," she murmured, ashamed. Later, as she talked, after we'd drunk the tea, I understood what memory had struck her. That was when they had had the first sign of Eddie's illness, but they had not understood it at the time—when he had slipped on the stairs, the hot water spilling over him.

She sat there, the used dishes on the table, idly stirring her spoon sometimes in the remainder of tea at the bottom of her cup. She told me everything that had happened to Eddie since I had seen him last. At times it seemed she must be speaking of somebody else. I couldn't see cheerful, good-natured Eddie changing so much. Once or twice I said something patiently about Mr. Raphel. But Syb said,

"People don't always understand what they're doing. Even grownups don't. Even very smart grownups."

"No. Of course not. He didn't mean anything like that to happen, I know. But—." There I stopped. "How is your mother?" I was almost afraid to ask that. "I brought her these." I handed Sybil the wrapped corsage.

"Poor Mama! She broke up for a while. She cried all the time. She's been resting—at a little place in the country,—a boarding house, but very nice people, a nice middle-aged couple run it, and they take care of her. They're very fond of her, and she loves the country. It's quite near here, and we take turns on Sundays going to visit her. She might be able to come home before winter . . . Thanks for the flowers. I'll put them in a vase when I get home."

"Well,—let's have the pastries now!" The waitress, smiling, brought us a tray with marzipan-covered cakes made to look like fruits and vegetables—pears, peaches, potatoes, tomatoes, oranges.

"Oh, they're too pretty to eat!" Sybil smiled, with a flash of her old gaiety, balancing her fork in her hand.

"All right. We'll frame them. Or trim a spring hat with them. Or—" I pretended to be thinking of other ways, then Sybil laughed and put a "pear" on her plate and broke it with her fork. She tested it. "Um-um!"

I put a "potato" on her plate, too.

"Oh, no, Hal—"

"*Carpe diem*," I said. "Enjoy the present moment."

"It reminds me—sometimes when Ed's salary had an extra in it—holiday bonus, or overtime, or such— he'd take me to a restaurant on Lenox Avenue. His friend Bob from the office would come with a girlfriend. She was smart, and Bob was a great joker, and we'd have such fun!

Once, we'd seen a movie, one of the old Walter Scott romances.

"And we had an idea, just for the fun of it, to work out a heraldic shield for the restaurant, with the motto, '*Iterum Edimus*,' 'Again We Eat,' with liver steak, couchant, *gules*, flanked with French fries, rampant, *or*, on a field *vert* signifying the spinach—"

We were both laughing, but then Sybil said, with a deep sigh, "How strange it would seem—I mean if one who has died should come back when we were talking about him—could come back,—and then would see us—*laughing*. Would he understand? I've noticed—at funerals,—an hour or so later,—the ones who loved him best—could be—laughing. Would the dead one know, do you think, that it was just *because* the sorrow was true, and deep,—or would he rush away, and feel himself forgotten?"

"You know the answer to that, Syb." I said. And then because she began to look thin and tense again, I exclaimed,

"Look, Sybil. Are you allowed to go anywhere yet? I mean,—is it Jewish law that you have to wait—I mean, how long before you can go out anywhere?"

"I don't know, Hal."

"Well,—you ask your father. Then—wait a minute, I've got to work this out. Mom and Dad have a Wednesday matinee subscription to the opera—it's only Dress Circle—"

"Opera!" Her eyes opened twice as large, and they glowed.

"They don't go every time, you know. I'll get them to give me their tickets some Wednesday."

"*Oh!* Oh, *Hal!*"

"Look up the programs; see if there's one you specially want to hear."

At their house, she urged me to come up.

"Unless," she said, "you don't feel like seeing my father. But, he *has* changed, Hal. Really."

"I don't feel anything against him, Syb. Fathers are people. My Dad used to say, when I said anything about Mr. Raphel,—he'd say, 'Hold your horses, boy. If he didn't care about his family, he wouldn't *be* there, working for them.' Maybe he couldn't carry all that trouble."

"That's what *he* says, too, now. He says the school took up so much of him he was never able to catch up with all he had meant to do for Eddie. So he had sort of given up on it. Hoped the time would come, and all that. He did buy a strip of land in Palestine for him. He's put it in Lilie's name now. Never be worth anything, but—it's a sign."

I came upstairs with her. I couldn't believe my eyes. Mr. Raphel had actually set the table for tea, with four cups and saucers, four forks and four spoons, and was setting down four plates. The cookies were spread out on a platter. He, who had always scorned to touch with his man's hands anything having to do with women's work!

He explained, a bit self-conscious, even a bit ashamed before me, I think.

"Lilie will be coming home any minute from her class. She is always tired at this time, finds tea refreshing."

"You're not at the school now, sir?"

"Oh, I have taken a Sabbatical leave. A change of work is a good thing. I am spending a year working with a group of scholars who are compiling a Hebrew-English modern dictionary. The salary is not high—"

"Naturally," put in Sybil, but she laughed.

"Don't you miss your pupils, Mr. Raphel?"

"They come to see me, from time to time."

"Papa," said Sybil, after a pause, "Hal might be able to get tickets for the opera. Can I go? I mean— is it required, by Jewish law,—to wait?"

Mr. Raphel's brows began to contract and his eyes to snap in the old way, but he stopped. He said, slowly,

"The Law . . . The Law is to *live* by." He paused

182

a long while, his eyes dull and far away. Then he came to, and looked at us again, and said, with some difficulty.

"I think there will be the opera *La Juive,* next month. If you go to that, I would like to know what the story is about."

SULAMITH ISH-KISHOR was born in London, where several of her poems were published by the time she was ten. After settling with her family in New York City, she studied history and languages at Hunter College. Always a prolific writer, Miss Ish-Kishor has contributed articles to many magazines, including the *New Yorker, Saturday Review, Reader's Digest,* and *The New York Times Magazine.* Her books include the popular CHILDREN'S HISTORY OF ISRAEL, AMERICAN PROMISE, A BOY OF OLD PRAGUE, (chosen as the outstanding children's book of 1963 by the Jewish National Book Council of America) and THE CARPET OF SOLOMON.